Seeing Zoey

Margaret Hertel

PublishAmerica

Baltimore

First printing

ISBN: 1-59129-913-6
PUBLISHED BY PUBLISHAMERICA BOOK PUBLISHERS
www.publishamerica.com
Baltimore

Printed in the United States of America

This book is dedicated to my one and only...always and forever.

I would like to thank my family and friends for their continuing patience and support.

1

"Five o'clock!"

Nora couldn't wait to get out of the office. To get away from the discipline of work, and be free of the compulsion to behave in front of others just as though life was normal and everything fine. Putting on an act had become a burden…and she needed out.

Walking to her car, she called Gabriella's direct line from her cell phone. Gabriella was still at her desk – hard at it.

"Hey!" Nora hoped she sounded casually breezy.

"Oh. Hi…" Gabriella answered distractedly. Then through clenched teeth she added, "What's up?"

"What's up is, I'm on my way to Fountains to meet Zoey for dinner. She's in a seminar and she doesn't know how long she can stay."

"And so?"

"So," Nora took a deep breath, "if she has to get right back and it's still early, can I come over? We need to talk."

Gabriella sighed, "Nora, am I supposed to be thrilled to be your backup plan tonight? Right in line behind your ex?"

"I only meant, well, I really do need to talk to you. I know you're mad, honey, and hurt. But I'm desperate. I miss you."

"Good, you should. And don't call me honey. I don't want to see you. I still feel like shit. I have to be in court early tomorrow and I'm not ready. Talking to you or even thinking about you is not going to help me."

"All right," Nora managed, in spite of a sudden ache in the back of her throat. "I'll come by tomorrow then, after you've left. I need to get some more things."

"You going to continue to stay with Sybil?"

"I guess. For the time being anyway, until I decide, uh, I mean we, decide if I should get my own place."

"Well, start looking." Gabriella's voice turned to ice. "I've already decided."

"Shit, Brie, four years? Just down the tube? You don't even want to try to fix this?"

Gabriella was silent for so long that Nora began to think she had hung up on her. Then she heard her inhale sharply and knew Gabriella was crying. "Nore...I love you. You know I do. God help me, but I do. I love you but you aren't worth it. I'm torn up inside. Nothing is worth feeling like this."

"But I love you, too. I told you I don't even care about Alison. Not the way I care about you." Nora started to cry then too, sitting in her car, her forehead pressed against the steering wheel. "Please, Brie...just give me a chance. I'll get counseling, that's why I'm seeing Zoey tonight."

"Oh, that'll be helpful. Your ex lover...she'd be the perfect shrink for you."

"Brie, it's been almost five years. And yes, she does know my issues, but I just want to get some names from her. See who she thinks would be good for me. She wouldn't see me anyway, even if I wanted her to."

"I know. Think she'd see me? I'm the one who's dying here. I'm the one who aches every time I take a breath, who can't concentrate and bursts into tears several times a day."

"I'm sorry, honey. I am so sorry," Nora cried into the phone. "If you're trying to make me feel worse than I do, give up. I can't! I can't possibly feel any worse. What can I say?"

"What is there to say?" Gabriella blew her nose. "Stay away from me for a while, Nora. I have to get my head together. Don't come over when I'm home and don't call at night after nine. I might have to take a sleeping pill tonight."

"Brie, don't do that! You know how I hate those."

"Tomorrow is big, Nora. Really big, and I haven't slept worth a damn for the last week. And you know what? You don't have a say anymore. No say, no way. What you like, or what you don't like, doesn't count."

"That...is...just...brutal," Nora sobbed, clutching her stomach.

"Have a good dinner with Zoey," Gabriella sobbed back. A sarcastic sob, if there is such a thing.

"I'll call you later."

"Not after nine. Oh, and don't forget your mail tomorrow, and get your damn messages off the machine. Three of them are from Alison. You might at least let her know you've moved out."

"I did already," Nora interrupted.

"And why does that piss me off?" Gabriella yelled furiously into the phone and hung up.

Unable to cope, Nora just lost control. When she finally looked into the rear view mirror, she confirmed that she looked just like she felt: awful! "Should I try to go home first and redo my face before dinner?" she asked herself. No. Then she'd be late, and maybe Gabriella would come home before she left.

She decided to just go to Fountain's ladies' room to repair at least the major damage. There was no point in making a huge effort for Zoey anyway, she'd get the true picture in a nano-second. She always did.

Nora parked in the lot, went in the front door and all the way to the rear to the ladies' room. Zoey hadn't arrived yet. While the cold water didn't do a lot for her makeup, it did reduce some of the swelling around her eyes. It also provided enough of a frigid jolt to stop the tears, at least temporarily. On her way toward the front, she chose a table for two, dimly lit, between the two large fountains that dominated the restaurant. She knew from experience that if you sat too close to either fountain, you ended up having to scream at each other.

She didn't have to wait long. They were supposed to meet at six and Zoey arrived ten minutes early. She wore a short-sleeved, light blue cashmere sweater, which was exactly the same color as the cardigan thrown over her shoulders, exactly the same color as her enormous blue eyes. Her pants were navy and tight, showing off her body. Her hair was short again, which Nora thought made her eyes look even bigger. Nora's breath caught in her throat, as it always did at first sight of Zoey. She raised her eyebrows. "You're early, a welcome surprise."

"Well, I was simply bored to death. They canceled tonight's meetings; the session finished at five. I figured you'd be here…that you'd come directly from the office and you'd be out of there, at five, like a shot, as usual." Zoey smiled, and dropped her purse on the floor as she sank into her chair. "But if you weren't here, I was purposefully prepared to drink alone. What a day. Boring doesn't do it justice. More like paralyzing, 'analysis paralysis,' that's what I'm suffering from. Self medication is in order." She swiveled her head around until she caught the waiter's eye.

"Absolute martini…dirty." She looked at Nora while she said it.

A little startled, Nora nodded.

"Two." Zoey grinned at the waiter…it was incandescent. It was that grin that always got to Nora. It lit up the room, the world, life, whatever. It came on so suddenly. A surprise, exposing bright, white teeth, igniting like a spotlight. And like a spotlight, it brightened all in its range.

"So how are you, Nora? You don't look as terrible as you sounded." Zoey zeroed in for the first time, blue eyes calm and assessing but ready in an instant, with a mischievous twinkle or a bellicose glare.

"I'm…uh, broken up," Nora whispered morosely.

"So I hear."

"You heard? But that's impossible. We haven't told anyone."

"Correction, darling. You haven't told anyone. Roxanne was in my discussion group this morning. She's playing bridge at Sybil's tonight. They were all informed that you might be there and that if you were, to keep it light and cheery and not to mention Gabriella. Besides, Gabriella told me herself about a week ago."

Nora was astounded. Totally amazed. "You're kidding."

"Get real. Join the real world. When was the last time you phoned your mother?"

"Why does that matter?"

"It matters, because your mother kept calling you at home and you were never there. She thought Gabriella sounded funny on the phone, so she called me. She asked me if I had seen you lately and if I knew what was going on. So I called Gabriella."

Their drinks came and Zoey paused for a sip. Nora did the same.

Their eyes met as Zoey dropped her voice. "She was a mess, Nora. Just a wreck. Could barely even speak. It was Sunday night and she said she hadn't even been dressed since Thursday. Took Friday off."

"Gabriella always takes Friday off," Nora commented, more sarcastically than she meant to. Zoey gazed at her, chin down, eyes peering over reading glasses that weren't there, peering right into her soul. "You going to tell me what happened?"

"I guess, if you want me to. What did Gabriella tell you?"

"Nothing. I wouldn't let her get into it. Kept it all about her, how she was getting along. That seemed to satisfy her."

"But then, if you knew…if you knew all this time, knew how I must be feeling, why didn't you call me?" Nora's feelings were hurt and her voice whined unpleasantly in her own ears.

Zoey leaned forward on her elbows. "Against the rules, Nora. I was waiting for you to tell me yourself. I didn't want to know anything about it until you were ready to tell me. It wasn't up to Gabriella. She didn't mean to tell me but I caught her at a bad time. A really bad time."

2

Nora and Zoey sipped at their drinks and checked out the menu. "How is your mom? She sounded so uncomfortable on the phone: 'sorry to bother me,' 'didn't want to keep me,' that sort of thing. I tried to chat, put her at ease. But I knew she couldn't wait to hang up. Funny, I didn't even realize that I missed her until I heard her voice again." Zoey's voice trailed off.

"She's fine. Dad too. How about yours?"

"She's fine. He's crackers…can't hear. Short term memory is a memory. Thank God for Joan, the good sister. I call her St. Joan. What about your sister?"

"Bonnie the breeder? She's going for family champ; two kids and knocked up again." Nora took a gulp of her drink. "It keeps Mom and Dad happy and busy, though, and off my back."

Zoey rolled her eyes. "She said wistfully."

"I wasn't being wistful. I don't do wistful."

"Okay, longing, desirous, melancholy…whatever. Just typical reactions – Erikson's 'Theory of Generativity' – the impulse as we age, to do things more worthwhile, like having a family. Plus, of course the tick, tock of your biological clock." She flashed Nora the grin again. "So now, tell me what's making you look and act so miserable, honey."

"Okay." Nora sighed and the back of her throat ached more. "I'll try, Zoe. I don't know if I can without getting too emotional and I don't want to cry, not here. First of all, remember Dinah Dickinson?"

"Your friend from L.A. – big girl – she stayed with us for a few days."

"Exactly. She's married now…has a son, about two or three. Well, she has had her suspicions about her sister, Alison, for a long time, thought she might be gay. Alison was coming here for a convention, so Dinah called me to ask if I could maybe meet her, have lunch or something. I don't know, I guess she thought it would be good if she could meet a real, live deviate and discover that we're not all that creepy. I said, 'Sure!' even though I really didn't want to. I don't know what I was expecting, another Dinah, I guess. I went to her hotel to meet her. She must have seen a picture of me – because she came right over and introduced herself. I was just blown away. God! What a gorgeous girl...blond hair, short like yours, but lighter, the way yours used to get in the summer."

"When I was younger and occasionally went outside in the daylight," Zoey threw in.

"Uh...yeah. Well, she lives in the San Diego area now. Does a lot of sailing." Nora began to eat her salad while continuing her confession. "We hit it off right away. I knew she was attracted and I suppose I was, too. Nothing big, just that she was so gorgeous. We had lunch, spent the afternoon sightseeing together and I took her took her home with me to meet Gabriella. I fully intended to take her back to the hotel after dinner but, well, we got into the wine and decided she had better stay in the guest room. You know Gabriella, into bed by nine during the week. Well, I uncorked another bottle..."

"I should have never introduced you to wine. Should have left you as I found you: a simple, naïve but comely, beer-guzzling wench. But since I did, shall we?"

Nora nodded and Zoey examined the wine list. "We're both having fish so, what do you think, the Chardonnay?" she pointed to her favorite, the non-pronounceable Grgich.

"We sat up until one o'clock in the morning, talking. She's really mixed up; has had several disastrous love affairs; can't believe she could possibly be gay."

"And that's all impossible for you to resist, my little nurturer."

"Please don't Zoey, don't go there."

"Sorry, honey. I just can't help it sometimes, and it might do you some good to recognize some foundational motivation."

"Anyway, she's so beautiful, but so mixed-up and so young. She reminded me of myself."

"How old is she?"

"Twenty-six."

Zoey laughed out loud. "Pilfering the playpen, are we not?"

"It's funny you of all people would say that. There's a six-year difference.

Same as with you and me."

Zoey nodded and became contrite. "I'm sorry, that wasn't fair. I think I'm, well I think I'm a little jealous. This girl is so gorgeous and so young, and her hair is like mine used to be..."

"You dumped me, remember?"

Zoey looked down. She fiddled with the diamond band on her left hand; the one Nora had given her.

"Doesn't Kirsten object to you wearing that?" Nora had to ask.

"Not really. I always wear it to conferences and seminars. I call it my flea collar, keeps the pests away. Besides, Kirsten is still upstate. She's trying to finish her play. Won't come back until it's done, she said."

"She's still the love of your life?" Nora hoped that she didn't sound bitter.

Zoey ignored that while the waiter returned with their wine. He poured some in a glass and she tasted it, taking the responsibility quite seriously. She swirled her glass and swirled some wine around in her mouth. She finally nodded to the expectant waiter who reacted as though he had won a prize. In triumph, he filled both of their glasses. As soon as he left, Nora tried again.

"So, is Kirsten still the love of your life?"

"I heard you the first time, Nora, and chose to ignore it. I didn't come here to talk about myself or Kirsten or the two of us together. Suffice it to say that I am happy with the way things are and I have made a commitment."

"Yeah. I know all about your commitments." Face it, Nora was bitter.

"If you're going to keep at it, I'm going to leave. We've been down this road before. We need to get it behind us," said Zoey levelly. Then she reached across the table and took Nora's hand. "I know you're in pain. That's why I'm here. Talking about us won't help."

"I know, I know," Nora whispered, "where was I?"

"You were up at one in the morning with the beautiful, young towhead." Zoey flashed that grin again.

"Yeah, well we talked. One thing led to another. Soon she was crying on my shoulder. I held her in my arms and sort of patted her on the back. She was just melting down. Her lips found my neck and she kissed me. But then she left them. Left them there, touching my neck. It was so sensuous, so arousing. I pushed her gently away, stood up and said, something like, 'You'll feel better in the morning. Anything you need? Goodnight.' Then I went upstairs. I saw her watching me go up the stairs. Her face was so full of longing. Just raw hunger. I should have known then."

"What about Gabriella? Wasn't she upset that you stayed up so late?"

"No, not at all. That happens almost every time we entertain. Even on the weekends, she bails early. Always by ten thirty. No, if anything, she was pleased." Nora began to blush. "I was so turned on by the time I got in bed, I woke Brie up and made passionate love to her."

Zoey nodded. "Trying to prove to yourself that you weren't having the feelings you were feeling. So far it doesn't sound so bad, Nora. Fairly typical, I would say, nothing totally 'abhorrent.'"

This was a little joke Zoey and Nora had shared. Once, when Nora was attempting to quote Zoey, Nora said someone's behavior was totally abhorrent instead of aberrant. Then, agreeing that it was indeed more loathsome than it was deranged, they laughed hysterically. 'Abhorrent' had been a special word with them ever since.

"I haven't gotten to the abhorrent part yet," Nora muttered. "By the time I woke up the next morning Brie had left. She left me a note, with one rose. "Thank you for last night. I love you so much. You're my everything." Nora clutched at her stomach, feeling that pain begin. "Alison and I decided to go out to breakfast before I took her back to the hotel. Then, once we got in the car, she asked if maybe we could go to her hotel first so she could freshen up. I said sure, she had on the same clothes as the day before, hadn't even brushed her teeth. So I called the office to check my messages while Alison popped into the shower. I noticed the red light on her phone was blinking, and when she came back into the room wrapped in a towel, I pointed it out to her. She called down to the desk. The message was from the most recent guy, Alvin or Albert, whoever. He's 'Mister Right,' the perfect guy, but she just can't make herself care. He was crying and said, 'Please don't do this, please call me.' She just came unglued... hysterical."

"And you took her in your arms, attempting to comfort her, as the towel she was wearing fell to the floor."

Nora stared at Zoey. "How did you know?"

"How did I know? It's my job, Nora. More importantly, how did you know and when did you know?"

"I don't know what you mean." Nora looked at her.

"I mean that you knew perfectly well what would happen when you went up to that girl's room with her. Perhaps you didn't know exactly, but you had a pretty good idea."

"I guess," Nora admitted, massaging her neck, "it's so scummy though. Something I never thought I'd do. Not after what happened with...I'm sorry," she whispered, as the tears returned and she began to lose control.

16

"Let's get out of here." Zoey stood up and threw some money on the table between their half-eaten entrees. drained the last of her wine, finished Nora's and literally pulled her out the front door.

3

"Where's your car?" Nora looked over the lot for Zoey's Jaguar.

"In the shop; where it lives," Zoey replied with disgust. "I took a cab here. You'll have to take me home."

They got in the car and then, flashing back on her phone call with Gabriella, Nora pressed her forehead against the steering wheel again and lost it. "The thing is," she sobbed, "I had no control, Zoe. None…zero. I was holding her, comforting her. The next thing I knew we were all over each other. It was her first time with a woman. She was so joyful, exuberant, full of wonder. I just…" Nora opened her eyes and saw Zoey leaning against the car door, facing her. Tears were running down her cheeks.

"What is it?"

"It just hurts me to see you like this. I know how you beat yourself up."

"And you know, because you've been right where I am." The minute she said it Nora was sorry.

"I suppose that's true and I suppose I deserve that. The irony is that Gabriella will feel the same way about you as you feel about me. All the hurt and bitterness betrayal brings. There doesn't seem to be any way to get over it. I've been trying for what, five years?"

"Almost, I guess." Tears still ran unchecked down Zoey's face and dripped off her jaw. She shrugged and held her arms out. Nora crawled over the personal console and gearshift. It was pure instinct.

They held tightly to each other. Zoey's voice was low. "You're so good, so good and pure, Nora. You hold yourself to such a high standard. When something like this happens, you self-destruct. You know what you did. You crossed the line. You got caught up in this girl's drama. You felt her pain.

You reached out to comfort her and then you crossed the line. You got turned on and swept away by passion. It happens every day in the lesbian world. It happens because our lovers and our friends come from the same group. Sometimes it's hard to know who is who. And sometimes someone starts out in one category and ends up in another. Half of my practice is a result of that damn line. So you made a mistake. The girl went back to San Diego, didn't she? Just try to forgive yourself and move on."

"It's not that simple, Zoey. It's more abhorrent," Nora sniveled. "I don't think Gabriella will forgive me. I know she'll never trust me again. She has such a problem with trust to begin with. Now, well I've just decimated any future possibility of it completely." She continued to cry, getting Zoey's sweater damp.

"Oh, I don't know Nore. Give it time. You trust me again," Zoey whispered into her hair.

"No I don't!" Nora sobbed. "Not like I did. I trust you as a friend…but in a relationship? How could I?"

"I'm sorry. God, I am just so, so sorry!" Zoey blinked, fighting back more tears.

"That's exactly what I said to Brie on the phone before I met you tonight."

"Take me home, honey. The door handle is sticking me in the back."

"I don't want to move. I like it here…our arms around each other. We never touch each other any more. Only quick embraces at the door arriving or leaving. I should say something about how wrong that feels, but that's your line." Nora shot Zoey another look, then climbed back behind the wheel. She blew her nose and started the engine. Then she picked tiny hairs off the tip of her tongue. "Cashmere," she sniffed, "I'm allergic." She added unnecessarily.

"Come in," Zoey said when they got to her place. This was neither an invitation nor a request. "I still haven't heard the abhorrent part, and it's still early." Nora hesitated, "And you need to wash your face."

That did it. Nora followed her inside. The place was the same as when she lived there. Only the guest room, which they had pretended was Nora's room, really was the guest room. The kitchen and dining area had that non-lived in, model home feel, an accurate assessment, as Zoey never cooked. Nora followed Zoey into the kitchen. She got out a bottle of wine and they examined each other in the harsh kitchen light.

"You look good Zoe, in spite of the mascara all over your face."

"And you look beautiful. Even more beautiful in your tragic suffering."

"Don't make fun, Zoey."

"I'm not, honey. I mean it. I've never seen your eyes as violet as they are right now."

"Probably because of my top." Nora's shirt was deep pink with long full sleeves and an open neck with a plunging neckline. She loved to wear it with her Tommy Hilfiger brown suede jeans.

"Maybe, honey, but the color is amazing what ever the reason."

"They probably pick up some from the deep purple circles under them, too," Nora groused.

Zoey dampened a clean towel, wrung it dry and carefully wiped Nora's face with it. "I like what you've done with your hair, too. It's so dark, it's practically black. A rinse? Or a dye?"

"Are you kidding? Look at all the gray! This is just my winter color. You aren't the only one whose hair gets lighter in the summer."

"I didn't notice any gray." Zoey turned from her task of opening the wine for a closer inspection.

Nora flicked her hair behind her ears on both sides. "Check out these babies."

A hand on each of Nora's hips, Zoey shook her head and made her clucking sound. "One or two, honey. Get a grip."

They sat on the sofa, their wine glasses and the bottle on the coffee table. "So shoot. Her towel falls to the floor, you jump her bones. What am I missing?"

Nora got up and made a fire. Mostly for something to do, but also because she didn't want to look at Zoey while she told her what it was that she was missing. She lit a match, sighing and remembering. "She was just incredible. I told you it was her first time with a woman – well she was on fire. Couldn't get enough of me; just wanted to keep on and on; wouldn't let me stop. She blew off the convention. Didn't even explain her absence. We put out the Do Not Disturb sign and made love until five that afternoon. She was crazed and I was too, I could hardly tear myself away. I couldn't believe it was me. I was full of regret and shame and self-loathing, but still I was unable to stop. I was crying and sick to my stomach and still couldn't stop. Finally, it scared me. I was so out of control. I told Alison, 'Goodbye forever,' and I really meant it. I was shaking all over by the time I got in my car. I could hardly drive home."

Zoey sat with her knees up in front of her, hands clasped around them. "I'd forgotten how you get." Her grin lit up the stratosphere. "How sex energizes you. Sounds like you met your match."

Nora sat down on the sofa with a thud. "If you've forgotten that then you've forgotten a whole lot. Alison's not the first one I've spent the entire day making love to, you know."

"I didn't really forget," Zoey admitted. "Nor am I likely ever to forget. It's just something I haven't let myself think about recently."

"I could hardly drive home, like I said. Brie and I had an early dinner and a soak in the hot tub."

"I'll bet," Zoey laughed

"And the whole time I was fantasizing about Alison. I got up in the morning when Brie did, kissed her goodbye and went directly to Alison's hotel. I knocked on her door a little after eight. She was stunned. I guess she really thought she'd never see me again. Then it was the same as the day before. We made love until two, when she had to leave for the airport. I'll spare you the details."

"I know the details, Nora, I know all of the details," Zoey sighed.

"And I've been fantasizing about it ever since. She was just so fresh and honest and she enjoyed it so much."

"And she was everything that Gabriella isn't," Zoey added.

"Well, it's almost medicinal with Gabriella," Nora reflected. "Once she's um, satisfied. No matter how quickly that happens, she's done."

"It's her age, honey. A natural manifestation of the aging process. Kirsten is the same. Unless she's really passionate about what she's working on. When that happens, she's likely to be passionate about everything. Including sex."

"Well, I'm not sure what all I said to her. What I said didn't matter by then anyway. She's been calling ever since, like ten times a day."

Zoey smiled. "Remember how we used to do that? On our phones all day; 'now what are you doing?'… 'getting in the shower'…'Okay call me when you get out.' That's just new, honey, it'll wear off. That is if the relationship continues. Is that what you want? For it to continue?"

Nora started to cry. "How can I want that? How can I and still be an honest, kind person. I need to get back with Gabriella. When I see her, or even think of her, I feel like such a shit. I gave her my word. I made a commitment, a solemn promise to her and then I betrayed her, broke my promise. You said yourself what a wreck she was."

"And that has what to do with Alison?"

"I don't know. I think I would like myself better if I could make it up to

Brie. It's probably not going to go anywhere, anyway, with Alison. She wouldn't want to leave San Diego. She's a marine biologist. I wouldn't want to go out there. I'm just getting my practice going."

"O.T.'s are in demand all over the country," Zoey put in.

"I know," Nora whispered.

"I know you know, honey." Zoey's voice was gentle. "Maybe Alison was just in the wrong place at the wrong time. Or is it the right place and the right time? Maybe this was a breakup waiting to happen."

"Why the hell would you say something like that?"

"'Cause I know you. You told me two years ago that Gabriella wasn't the one. You just couldn't get yourself out of it. Then, along came Alison. You used her to do the deed."

Nora was horrified and sick at the same time.

"Want me to prove it?" Dumbly, Nora nodded her head. Zoey sat back on the sofa and folded her arms. "How did Gabriella find out?"

"I don't want to tell you that." Nora shut her eyes and rubbed her aching neck.

"Why, too revealing?"

"Too abhorrent." Nora shook her head. "It was the worst thing, the single most terrible moment of my life." Then sobbing and choking, she held her head in her hands and went on. "It had just been a regular day, uneventful, and a regular evening. I went to bed when Brie did, and we made love. That's my signal to her that I want to. Otherwise I usually stay up a while and read. I mean, well nine o'clock? Every night? Anyway, we made love and it was good, really good. It always is with us. Brie held me in her arms afterwards and told me how much she loved me and I was so turned on. I wanted more. Brie was wiped, I could tell. So after a couple of kisses I gave up and let her go to sleep. She likes to do that right afterwards. If she doesn't, then it takes her a long time to drop off." Nora stood up and paced around. "Then I began to fantasize about Alison. She'd been gone about a week, I guess, and we were having intense phone conversations. So, I kept thinking about her, and about how different it was with her and I got so...so...."

"Horny," Zoey suggested.

"Uh...yeah. Honestly, I couldn't stand it. I got up, went down to the kitchen and called her from the kitchen phone. Brie woke up then, saw the light on the phone and picked up the receiver just in time to hear me whisper, "I want you so much right now that I can barely stand it."

Zoey stared at Nora a long time, her mouth slightly open. She was clearly appalled. Finally she said, "Oy!" Then, pouring them each more wine, "I do believe, Nora, that that is the very worst one I've ever heard. And as you can imagine, I've heard some dandies. However, it does prove my point."

4

Suddenly chilled, Nora stood with her back to the fire – awaiting the sharp edge of Zoey's scalpel that she knew was surely on its way. She waited. Zoey just looked at her.

Finally Nora blurted out, "So you think that I purposely wanted Brie to find out? That I wanted to hurt her like that? What kind of a monster do you think I am?"

"I don't think you purposely wanted to hurt her, at least not on a conscious level. You're too good and kind to want to do that. The fact is that you consistently put the other person first in your relationships. That's key because if you pursued a relationship with Alison, maybe by putting her needs first you could excuse your betrayal of Gabriella. Or partly excuse it. Then you could go on being an honest, kind person and still like yourself."

"I can't believe I could do that to Gabriella. The timing of it…having sex with her, and then…how could I do that Zoey?"

"How indeed. You must have realized the chance you were taking. It shows how desperate you must have been."

"You mean physically? That's not an excuse."

"You were desperate, Nore," Zoey told her gently. "You were desperate to get out. Who knows, is a swift dagger through the heart, well aimed and perfectly placed, preferable to small, random, puncture wounds that slowly, inevitably bleed you to death? You're so out of touch with your feelings, honey, and you don't deal with things when they come up. You repress everything to the back burner. You think those repression's remain, status quo, until you're ready to deal with them. But they don't, Nore. They grow and grow. Feed upon themselves exponentially. Then one day the burner is on overload. It can't hold anymore. It explodes and it's all overwhelming. You can't deal, so you act out. You let your actions take over, let them speak for you. Then, when others react to those actions, they have to take the responsibility for their reactions. It's their, fault then. That's how you avoid responsibility."

"Even if that's all true, even if that is the reason for what I did, the bottom line here is what I've done to Brie. I don't know how to fix it…make it better."

"But if I'm right, if the break up was inevitable, then how could you have done it without hurting her?"

"I don't know," Nora admitted after a protracted silence. "I guess there is no good way."

"Your guess is right, there isn't. That's why some of us lie, cheat and act as shitty as possible. Hoping the other person will break it off. That's also why some of us pretend that there's someone else. It's just easier than saying. 'I don't love you anymore,' or 'this isn't working for me, I want out.'"

Nora thought about it. Zoey was right, of course. She hadn't been really happy with Gabriella for a while. A long while. Not like she had been with Zoey. Then Nora got it. They faced each other. Showdown at the OK Corral.

"Is this a confession? Are you telling me that's what you did to me…to break up with me?" In spite of Nora's best intentions, she began to cry again.

Zoey looked down at her hands. "You have to believe me, Nore. I swear to God! I didn't know it. I've never even thought it, not until just now when I said it. I always told myself…I always thought I had fallen in love with Kirsten."

"It's true, though," Nora wouldn't let it go. "You used Kirsten to break up with me the same way I used Alison to break up with Brie."

"Not exactly. I never was unfaithful to you. I told you I thought I loved her and wanted my freedom so I could see her. At the time, that was all true."

"Okay, so you were more honorable. I'll give you that," Nora seethed. "But it didn't hurt any less."

"And it wouldn't have hurt any less had there not been someone else," Zoey sighed.

Nora continued to cry and Zoey put an arm around her shoulder. "Tell me, can you tell me what it was? Why you wanted out?"

"Oh, Nore, don't. Don't go there. It was a lot of stuff. We were both in different places then. Some of the things that annoyed me the most are now the things I miss the most. Other things, things you used to do, you don't do anymore. What's the use of dragging through it all now?"

"Because I need to know," Nora stammered, still crying. "I need to know if it's something I did. I never did know why and I still don't. I mean, if it wasn't Kirsten, then you, of all people. You, with your great regard for the truth. You owe me that at least."

Nora knew just what buttons to push. A direct hit.

"Okay." Zoey stood up. "I'll try," she sighed. "Although I don't know if anything resembling closure is possible, if that's what you have in mind. Might as well get comfortable, I guess. You want to borrow some sweats?"

Nora hesitated, as she followed Zoey into her bedroom. Warning signals were going off in her brain. Not about the sweats; about the getting comfortable. She didn't know how comfortable she wanted to get with Zoey. Emotionally and mentally they were still intimate, but physically, well, that was an entirely different story. She had felt herself beginning to respond earlier when they were in the car and in each other's arms, so she was cautious. Scared of what might happen.

Zoey picked up on her ambivalence, but not the reason for it. "How perfect." She looked at Nora, fists on her hips. "There was a time when I couldn't get you out of sweats. Now look at you, designer jeans?"

"Hilfiger," Nora shrugged.

"And what you had on last month at that concert?"

"Dana Buckman," Nora nodded. "Well Gabriella likes good clothes. And she likes me to wear them and I, well I've learned to appreciate the difference."

"I'm not criticizing you, Nora. It's just another one of the ironies, and one of the ways we've both changed.

"This feels so weird. Talk about wrong!" Nora looked around at Zoey and Kirsten's things, commingled and cohabiting.

"It feels weird, honey, because it is weird." Zoey assured her, handing her some blue sweats. She went in to the john and Nora absently picked up a three by five manila card. The paper stock was heavy and the sketch on the front was freehand – very Picasso – a few spare lines.

It was a woman's face and obviously Zoey. She still held it when Zoey came back into the room."Where did this come from, Zoe? It's good!"

"I know, too good. Turn it over."

On the back, Nora read, "The peace and quiet envelope me relentlessly, serving as a constant reminder of what I came up here to escape. It seems I no longer even need you to be obsessed and consumed by you."

"I better call her right now," Zoey decided, snatching the card from Nora's hand. Waving it in the air, she continued, "this is my jaw line. She adores my jaw line, just adores it! But, when she spends this much time on something, refining and polishing, it means she's stuck. Having a white-out, a writer's block. This arrived yesterday. Hopefully, she's past it by now. You don't mind do you?"

"Of course not. She goes to bed early too?"

"No, honey. She starts work about nine; works until five or six in the morning; sleeps until three. That's one reason why we don't live together."

"Oh, I didn't know. I just assumed you did."

"No, we need our own space. Besides, she has a mother and a dog, both of whom I'm allergic to." Zoey picked up the cordless phone. "This damn base unit is permanently stuck on speaker-phone. I can't get the button to pop up to turn it off."

Nora heard the phone ring through the speaker in the base unit and went to the john to give Zoey more privacy. Kind of a formality because she could still clearly hear the entire conversation.

"Hi, honey, how are you?"

"I'm okay. Better. Just about to sit down at my desk."

"That's what I figured. I got your note. It's beautiful. I treasure it."

"Then its purpose was achieved! I thought it came out well. I was pleased with the result."

"How's the play coming, honey? Everything okay?"

"You have mystic powers, my love. The final scene is finished. Carved in stone. And it's good Zoe, really really good. But it wasn't where I was going when I began. So," Kirsten sighed, "I have to re-write parts of Act One and probably deep six the whole second act."

"Are you sure?"

"Fairly sure. It'll be worth it though, for the new ending."

"And when did you do that?"

"Last night. Did I tell you that Reecie is up here?"

"Reecie Baldwin?"

"In the flesh. She just finished taping the last episode of her series, the last ever. She came up for a rest. She wants to do something with me. We haven't worked together for years. Not since her first series. She wants to do a play next, she said. So I showed her what I have. We kicked it around a little and I rewrote the end for her. It was grand, Zoey. It just came pouring out of me. It was scintillating, moving, just fabulous stuff. Reecie has such insight, such emotion. I had forgotten how we meshed together. How we just clicked. I'm so newly impassioned!"

"Well, that's great! Just great! Has Reecie read it yet? You think she'll like it?"

"She was here when I wrote it, Zoe. I scribbled out page after page on my yellow tablet and handed it to her. She was totally impressed; called me a genius."

Then Nora heard a slight change in Zoey's voice. "Reecie's there? At your place?"

"Of course. Where else would she be? There's nothing around here but homes. No inns or hotels. That doesn't bother you, I hope."

"Don't be silly, I trust you. You know how I feel about trust. Without trust..."

"Zoey, you're not alone, are you? I can tell by your voice."

"It's only Nora. She and Gabriella are having problems."

"Oh, super. Only Nora!" Kirsten went ballistic.

"How like you, going for the role reversal. You're the one with the house guest."

"We are working, Zoey."

"So, what the hell do you think I'm doing? I told you Nora and Gabriella are having problems."

"Hello! Nora and Gabriella have always had problems. Or at least one problem."

"And that would be?"

"You, of course. Be the professional that you claim to be, Zoe, and admit that Nora has never gotten over you."

"Maybe. Maybe that's why I feel so responsible."

"If I thought all you felt was responsible I wouldn't care so much that she's there."

"What is that supposed to mean, K?"

"It means that you can't get past her. You still have her pictures everywhere. You cry when she's in pain and she always, always, God damn it, comes first. You figure it out. You figure out what it means. You're the shrink."

"I trust you, K, and I know you trust me. So let's stop all this. I guess I'm a little jealous. Only because I miss you. I won't keep you any longer, honey."

Nora could hear the doubt in Zoey's voice. "I'm thrilled that it's going so well. Hurry and finish and return to me as soon as you can."

"You know I will. I love you Zoey." Kirsten's voice dropped a dramatic octave.

Nora returned from the john to the bedroom. Zoey was sitting on the edge of the bed, her elbows on her knees. She still had the cordless in her left hand and was lightly whacking herself on the top of her head with it.

Their eyes met as Nora entered the room. She didn't think Zoey realized that she had heard the whole conversation, from both ends. Nora didn't know what to say or even what to think about it, so she pretended she hadn't heard it. She excelled at doing that.

5

"If you really insist on getting into this, I'm going to open another bottle of wine," Zoey warned, "and you are not driving all the way to Sybil's."

Nora was surprised. Another bottle? This was not like Zoey. "Okay. I better call her and tell her."

"Don't tell her you're here for Christ's sake. It'll be all over town."

Nora nodded, and punched in the number. She could hear raucous laughter in the background as Sybil answered. "Hi Syb, It's me. Don't wait up for me. I'm not coming over tonight."

"Oookay, are you with Gabriella?" Sybil's voice came at her from the base unit in the bedroom, as well as the cordless receiver.

"Uh, no…"

"Oh, at Jeannie's?"

"No, no…"

"Marcie and June's?"

Nora looked at Zoey. "No…I…"

"You're with Bonnie?"

Zoey's eyes opened wide. "No, Syb, for Christ sake."

"Charlene…Charlene at the office?"

Zoey's eyebrows shot up and Nora exploded into the phone, "God! Sybil!"

"Oh, Nore, don't tell me, not Lanie, not again," Sybil whispered.

Nora just hung up and turned to face an astonished Zoey. She shrugged. "They're all just friends, in spite of what Sybil thinks."

They threw the pillows from the sofa onto the floor and settled there – in front of the fire. Nora started to hum, 'Seems like old times…'

"If you want me to tell you the truth Nore, then you're going to have to

31

help me. Try to understand. Try to get yourself out of it and come from my perspective. I don't want to upset you or hurt your feelings so if you start to get emotional, I'll have to stop. I don't understand why this is something you need to even know at this late date. Is it a self-improvement issue?"

"No," Nora said softly, "but I think you owe it to me. All this time I thought it was just because of Kirsten and now I find out it wasn't and, like I said, I need to know why."

"Well, there is no why. Not one thing, like bad breath," Zoey grinned. "It honestly was partly Kirsten, but it was also a lot of stuff. I don't know if I can even recreate it authentically, recapture where I was. I had finished my thesis, was in the middle of my post doc work, studying for my boards and working at the clinic part time for extra money. Every minute of every day was scheduled. Then I fell crazy in love with you. You were impulsive, undisciplined, carefree and irresistible. You were also counterproductive. The more I let you in, the more the rest of my life went down the tubes. The more time I spent with you, the guiltier I felt and the further behind I got. We never should have lived together. I'd come home at seven – seven thirty – exhausted and you'd have your swim club here for a barbecue. 'Hope you don't mind Zoey, spur of the moment.' And, what could I say? I didn't mind so much, really. I was glad you had friends and activities. I didn't have time to be with you that much and it took the pressure off me. But then, I had the choice of partying with you and not studying and then feeling guilty and hating myself for it, or locking myself upstairs, trying to ignore the party, and trying to study."

"I knew that," Nora stared into the fire, "but you told me to go ahead, have anyone over, whenever."

"I know, and I meant it, I'm just telling you now that it became a real issue with me. It started out fine, but you kept adding on more friends, joining more groups. It got to be too much. I'd be coming home, turn the corner, see a bunch of cars in front of the house and break into tears. If it wasn't the swim club, it was the ski club with their endless films, or the morons from that stable, or the band. Dear God! That band nearly drove me insane."

"I had no idea, Zoe! You were always so gracious and welcoming. I thought you liked all of them. Really, I did. I thought you wanted me to have them all come to our house because you didn't want me to be off somewhere else all the time. I didn't want to leave you alone, but I didn't want to sit around by myself and watch you study twenty-four hours a day, seven days a week, either. I thought it was a nice compromise. You'd join us for a little while, and then you'd disappear. And really, you acted like you liked everybody."

"Well, I did individually. It just all piled up on me. Something practically every night and I needed some down time. It got so I dreaded coming home. I felt old and crabby and tired and I couldn't help it. I didn't want to say anything to you, I guess, because I was afraid you would think I was the way I felt. I thought maybe you were reacting to the boring life style I lived. You were so young, so full of fun, so beautiful. The opposite of what I thought I was. What was perfectly appropriate behavior for you at your age was inappropriate for me. It just felt wrong. And what was appropriate for me bored you silly. I began to think that you were filling your life with others because you didn't want to be alone with me, that you were completely bored with me."

Staggered, Nora looked closely at her. Could she possibly have ever thought that? "I thought I was killing time. Killing time and filling time, until you passed your boards and finished your post docs and had time for me...for us." Nora was simply so stunned by the contrast between Zoey's viewpoint and her own, that she could barely say it aloud.

"Also, you were such a slob. I'd leave the house every morning, spotless and neat and I'd come home every night to a mess," Zoey frowned. "That made me crabby, too. Oh, you'd clean it up after I nagged at you, I just hated the nagging."

"I knew that, too. I tried to keep things clean but I got distracted. I'm just the opposite now. A total neat freak, now I'm always picking up after Brie. Was picking up after her, that is," Nora corrected herself glumly. "I still swim, but don't belong to the club anymore. Same with the ski club. I still see them once in a while."

"The thing that bugged me about all of them was that they were all coming on to you all the time."

"You're not serious Zoe. You thought that?"

"Thought it! They were blatant about it. Left nothing to the imagination. And you, you were so stupid, so oblivious. I used to wonder if you really didn't pick up on it or if you were faking it. Enjoying all the attention; flirting and leading them on."

"You have to be kidding. I can't believe you thought that! Like who, for instance?" Nora couldn't help it, she was irritated.

"Well, that Fredricka for instance."

"Freddie? From the stables?" Now Nora was dumbfounded. "God! Zoey! She's mentally challenged. Her parents own the place. She got kicked in the head when she was six. She has seizures and walks with a limp. When I first started riding there she wouldn't go near the horses. It took weeks for her mom and me to finally coax her up into the saddle. Then weeks more to get her to ride the horse at a slow walk around the corral. One of us had to lead him with the reins while the other walked next to her, holding her hand. After a while she began riding double, behind one of us."

Zoey held a hand up. "That's where I came in, at the fair."

"What?" Nora had not the slightest idea where this was going.

"For Christ's sake Nore! She had her hands either on your boobs or between your legs the whole time!"

"She was holding on."

"I'll say! She was practically drooling, too."

"I can't believe you said that. You, a member of the healing profession."

"Sorry. I'm sorry. I'm just trying to be honest."

"What's sad is, she does drool." Nora started to choke up. "And that was such a triumph for her that day." She wiped tears from her eyes.

"I'm sorry. God, Nore. I'm really sorry, but it was a big deal at the time to me. Then that girl on the ski team that got you so drunk you stayed on the mountain with her, instead of coming home on the bus with everyone else."

"I had to get an x-ray. I thought I broke my collarbone. I got drunk after I missed the bus."

"And I went to the Greyhound Depot at midnight to pick you up and you weren't on the bus. God! I was ticked! Then there were those behemoths on the swim team, always touching you, giving you rubdowns. And the band! Endless hours of rehearsing and practicing the guitar, with that bitch, Caroline."

"She was teaching me how to play," Nora protested, clearly annoyed.

"Every time I looked she was standing behind you with her arms around you."

Nora absolutely could not believe this. "And you thought…"

"I didn't know what to think. But the combination of your various activities and your, um, small army of admirers, and the day-to-day grind of my own life was disastrous. Sometimes I'd get so down, so dejected or discouraged and then you weren't there for me. I remember once after a miserable day evaluating small children who had been abused. All I wanted to do was hold you close and feel the comfort of your love. And you were in the garage rehearsing with the band. Then you fixed dinner for the gang at work."

"You never told me that, Zoe. I was trying to keep things light and carefree with something happening all the time. I thought that was what you wanted. I knew you were trying so hard not to bring the pain home from your work. I thought I was helping, distracting you. Allowing you to turn it off."

"I didn't want to turn it off, or cover it up. All I wanted was to let it out," Zoey said softly. "To hold you tight and cry if I had to. You just weren't mature enough to handle that in those days, so you created an environment where that could never happen."

Nora stared at her. This was a Zoey she had never seen before. "You must have wanted to say that for a long time. It takes some of the onus off you. But, if you'd only told me, I would have done anything, anything for you. All I ever wanted to do was to be there for you." As she said it, Nora realized how true it was and she cried yet again – mourning the loss of what they once had.

"If only I had told you," Zoey repeated bitterly. "You seem to forget how you were in those days. You refused to talk to me about anything like that. I'd bring up the subject, you'd ignore it and run away. I'd say, 'Nora, I want to talk,' and you'd say 'Well, I don't,' and you'd withdraw emotionally. I couldn't get you to trust me with your feelings. You wouldn't let me in. You wouldn't talk to me. After a while I gave up, but that was big, Nore."

6

Nora was getting more and more angry. "And that's it? That's why you broke up with me? I was scared, Zoey. Scared of you analyzing me. I didn't know what therapy was or what a therapist did. I was scared that if you found out what I was like, how insecure I was and how immature I was, that you would lose respect for me. Or you wouldn't love me anymore. I tried to always keep it light, not get deep. Therapy fixed that. You must have known it would, Zoe. So, because I wouldn't talk; a retarded, scared girl held on to me for courage; Caroline taught me to play the guitar; and some people gave me rubdowns. You must not have cared. You must not have ever cared that much if you could break up with me for such stupid, little…"

"Those were only examples, Nora. And it wasn't stupid or little. It was, in fact, constant and consistent. It was the way you were living your life. And you flirted with everyone, still do. The way you toss your hair back and wrinkle your nose when you smile. You suck them in, pull them to you, and then pretend not to notice when they hit on you. You do it with everyone! And then you claim that they're only friends. It used to make me crazy and then it made me think I was crazy!"

"But Zoey, they were only friends," Nora rolled over onto her back. "From the moment that we met I knew that you were the one, my one and only, and you always were. You were my lover. They were my friends. It was that simple. I never even thought of anyone else as a lover."

"Maybe not, Nore, maybe not. But that's not the way it came off, not to me. Your friends are lesbians. They're attracted to other women. You are a beautiful, attractive woman and they are attracted to you! They wouldn't be lesbians if they weren't."

Nora glared at her, the back of her hand pressed against her mouth. "Want me to prove it? Call Sybil back and ask her if she thinks anyone on the ski team was attracted to you, or anyone in your band. I'm serious. Here!" and she handed Nora the cordless phone.

Nora was upset but she was also sure that Zoey was way off base. She needed to prove something to herself and to Zoey, so she called Sybil. "Syb, hi, it's me again."

"Hi, 'me again.' You change your mind? Coming over after all? You must have had it with Diana. I figured that's where you were."

"No, I'm not coming over and I'm not with Diana."

"Then it's Megan...Megan for sure. I knew it had to be one or the other."

"I rest my case," Zoey whispered, laughing quietly.

"Syb, listen. Did you ever think anyone in that band I was in was, um, attracted to me?"

"Is this a joke? You're not smoking weed and hanging with them are you?"

"No, no. Nothing like that. Just reminiscing. I just wondered, you know."

"Anyone but them, honey." Sybil's voice became more confidential as she moved away from the bridge table. "Too folksy; definitely not our scene. As far as being attracted to you, well, that was the point of the whole thing, wasn't it? Goddess Nora and her four idolizers. Wasn't that your name?"

"Not the Idolizers. It was 'The Idylists' that means composers of idyls. Idyls are 'simple descriptions' – in prose or poetry – of rustic, simple life. That was the point of the band, Sybil."

"Well, whatever. They all had the hots for you."

Nora's stomach began to churn and she felt like she was going to be sick. "What about everybody else? Can you think of anyone else that, that maybe felt that way?"

"It'd be easier to answer that one backwards...like who hasn't had those feelings."

"And your point is?" Nora's head pounded and her eyes burned.

Sybil's voice became less sharp. "I just meant, that there's probably not a woman in this town, who's family, who hasn't been attracted to you at one time or another. Three of them are in my dining room right now, waiting for me, speculating about where you are and wondering, probably, if this is their chance."

"Uh...yeah. Better let you go, Syb, thanks." Nora couldn't get off the phone fast enough.

"So, are you writing your memoirs, or what? Oh, I know, you're with that bookstore owner. What's her name…Yvonne! Of course, how stupid of me."

Nora hung up and looked at Zoey. She sighed, "You're always right!"

"It's my job, Nore. It's what I do all day."

"What Sybil said about all those girls. She's so wrong. I never was unfaithful to Brie until now."

"I know. I know, you weren't."

"And I never was unfaithful to you, not ever. Never even tempted."

"I know that Nore," Zoey closed her eyes.

"Maybe you know it now. You didn't when it mattered." Nora was losing control. "You broke up with me because I made temporary messes that I always cleaned up and had people over to the house when you never – not even once – asked me not to. And you were jealous of everyone around me, everyone. Even poor Freddie. But mostly, I think you broke up with me because you thought of me like Sybil does. That I go around giving everyone the 'come on.' God! I can't believe I come off like that; so shallow and flirty. I hate that so much." Out of control, she cried and cried.

Zoey handed her a tissue. Like all pros, she was never without them. "I was insecure with you, too. That's why communication is so important and that's why I was so jealous. The only time you said you loved me was in the heat of passion. You always looked like you were having so much fun. You enjoyed your friends so much. Our time together was so limited and I resented always having other people around. Then, when we were alone it didn't seem like we ever had that same kind of fun. So I was jealous of that, too. I couldn't get you to talk, to open up to me. I thought it was because you didn't trust me with your feelings, and I didn't know how you really felt. It was self-preservation. I needed to know how you felt."

Nora couldn't believe it. "You didn't know how I felt? I bought you flowers and little presents and made you special dinners and packed your lunch with special surprises. I adored and idolized you. I made you fudge and chocolate chip cookies and I made love to you every chance I had. If I didn't laugh it up and make jokes and have that kind of fun with you when we were alone together, it was because I was so desperate to make love. We had so little time together. I sure didn't want to spend it doing anything else. I loved you totally and completely." She sobbed, in a fury. "I built my life around you and you ruined it…ruined my entire life."

Zoey was crying by then, too. Kirsten was right. She always did cry when Nora was in pain. "But you ate the fudge and the cookies, too. And as far as the sex was concerned, don't even try to pretend that you were only thinking of me. The problem was that you didn't tell me, Nore. You never once said, 'I love you!' When I said it to you, you always said, 'Thank God' or 'I'm so glad you do,' or something. It bugged me."

"I just had a hard time saying what I felt in those days. I thought my actions spoke loud enough about my feelings."

"Loud enough for some perhaps, but I'm a therapist, Nora. I need those words…the words that tell me you own your feelings."

"Maybe that was part of the problem."

Zoey looked at her, questioning.

"Sometimes I felt like I was on your couch. I guess I resented it. The more you prodded, the more I clammed up. It isn't easy living with a therapist, you know. You get to feeling like every little thing you do or say is being analyzed."

"At least you admit to being resentful and clamming up. At least I'm not completely the bad guy."

"No, therapy did help me there. That's what hurts the most now. You are a therapist, Zoey, every inch of you. And you believe in therapy. I just wish we would have had some, together or separately, before you broke up with me."

Zoey looked like she had been kicked in the stomach. "I think I like you better the way you were back then. When you wouldn't verbalize, pre-Roberta."

"If it wasn't for Roberta, I don't think I'd be here."

"Dramatic, but probably true in the strictest sense of the statement," Zoey grinned. "You probably wouldn't be here at this moment confiding and confessing."

"I don't know if I'd be here, period. I never really thought of killing myself, nothing like that. I just didn't want to be alive. Life sucked. I didn't think I had anything to live for and I didn't think I could believe in anyone or anything ever again. Roberta was tough. It was the hardest thing I've ever done, but she gets the credit. Do you think I should go back to Roberta, or should I see someone else?"

Zoey squinted and frowned. "I don't think you need to see anyone, Nore. You feel despondent and lonely, and your life is in upheaval and you despise yourself for the way you hurt someone who loved you. But those are all normal feelings, normal reactions to what occurred. And you certainly know why you feel the way you do. It isn't therapy that you need, it's time. The healing power of the passage of time."

"But I told Brie I would get counseling."

"Sure! That's what you told her. Because you want her to think that you have no clue why you did what you did…no explanation. It must be something deep within, something out of your control. Wait a few months. Then, when things have settled down, go back to Roberta if you think you need to."

"Yeah, that makes sense," Nora sighed. "I don't think I'm up for Roberta right now, anyway. Just the thought of telling her what I did scares the shit out of me."

Zoey stared into the fire, remembering. "Yes, Roberta was tough. Tough for me, too. I knew it would be when I recommended her, her office being right down the hall from me. But I also knew she would be the best person for you. I knew you saw her Tuesdays after work, and I knew you were her last appointment. I used to stay late every Tuesday. I'd sit at my desk and look down on the parking lot, waiting for the two of you to appear."

"Yeah. She usually left when I did."

"Sometimes the two of you would stand there a long time, close together, talking. Sometimes Roberta would touch your arm or give you a hug."

"You remember that?"

Zoey nodded slowly.

"Zoey, you are not going to tell me that you thought Roberta was hitting on me!"

"Of course not. I knew that there was probably a little transference occurring, but she's too professional to let anything happen. I was jealous of her though. I wanted to be her. Be standing in the parking lot with you, and have you talk to me like that. Watching you, the two of you, made me feel like such a failure. There she was, inside, where I couldn't go. It was real tough and then having her know what I did to you. That whole scene with Roberta was so difficult for me. Roberta knew it, too. She was able to see you, be there for you and not let it affect her relationship with me, professional or social. We both have a lot to thank her for. I bet I haven't even seen Roberta for over a year. Not since she moved her office out to the University."

"I talked to her a couple of weeks ago. She referred a patient to me, an accident case. She asked how you were. I said, fine, I guess. She was surprised that we aren't together. She saw us that time, having lunch, and I guess she thought…" Nora's voice trailed off.

Zoey frowned. "Roberta thought that, huh? Funny, so did Frank when he saw us shopping for shoes."

"We must have looked happy together."

"I suppose we did. And don't tell me you don't do 'wistful.'"

"I'm sorry. I just can't help thinking sometimes, of what might have been. It makes me feel so sad. Sad and hopeless." Nora's voice was barely audible.

"Join the club, honey." Zoey finished her glass of wine and poured herself some more. "We all think about what might have been and feel sad and hopeless," she raised her glass in a toast. "Here's to the newest member of the club...Gabriella."

Nora did not join her. She couldn't. She felt too sick inside. Instead, she rested her head on her crossed arms and went to pieces.

Zoey rubbed her back. "I'm sorry. That was harsher than I meant it to be. But that's where she is Nore, where she is right now."

"I know, and I know you were right about her. I did use Alison to get out of that, and that makes it even worse."

"Well that's only because Alison is not on the scene. If she were, then you'd have to become involved with her. You'd be madly in love for a while and at least you'd have a reason. A reason for Gabriella."

"The voice of experience? Like Kirsten was a reason for me?"

"Maybe that's true," Zoey nodded, "but not the way you mean it. My voice of experience comes from behind my desk. Hour after hour of hearing the same story. Who knows, maybe it affected how I behaved with you and Kirsten. It's cynical and it's not very pretty, Nore, But it's how things are. In our world, it's how things are. As far as me using Kirsten, well, if I did, I didn't see it like that at the time. Remember what I said to you when we broke up? I needed space and time. Time to decide if Kirsten and I were right for each other."

Nora sat up, not looking at Zoey. "I thought you really meant that. I thought you wanted my permission to see us both and that surely you would come back to me. But you didn't want to see us both at all. You had already decided." White-hot tears scalded her cheeks and ran down her face.

"Remember what else I said? That Kirsten really loved me, that she told me, over and over, every day, how much she loved me? Well, you were supposed to stand up and say that you loved me too. You were supposed to." Zoey wiped her tears with the back of her hands in frustration. "But you didn't. I felt...I felt then that I had my answer. That I finally knew the truth."

"I...I don't remember any of that. After you told me it was over, I didn't hear anything else. I was just so blown away, surprised, hurt, devastated, fatally wounded. After that, I felt dead inside. Nothing much registered."

7

"I was confused. I knew that I really did love you. But she just swept me off my feet. She was so flamboyant and powerful and brilliant and she made me feel all the things I didn't feel with you. With you I felt old. Mature and responsible, but also worn out and crabby. With Kirsten, I was the young one. Youthful, spontaneous, captivating and alluring. It was such a high. Such a change for me. I thought she was the one."

Zoey's voice softened. "She was everything you weren't: cerebral, challenging. I couldn't get you to open up, to tell me how you felt. She was the opposite. She revealed it all, every detail of every emotion, minutely and incessantly. She could go for days, rhapsodizing on the first time she saw me wear high heels or obsessing on how she felt when I let the box boy at the market carry our groceries to the car instead of having her do it."

"What?" That got Nora's attention. She stopped crying and, leaning on an elbow, looked over at Zoey in bewilderment. "How did she feel?"

"Dismayed, discarded, dismissed and discounted, her own words."

"No way!" Nora laughed. "That is just ridiculous!"

"True, but also clever, very clever. It got her out of going to the market. She has never gone with me since then. Couldn't bear to. It would open old wounds, she claims. It took me a while to figure it all out but Kirsten is a writer, a real, honest to God, writer. She would rather write about something than do it: eating, sex, listening to music, going to the movies, anything. She has written me love poems that are so beautiful that they bring you to tears, and others so passionate that they arouse you in an instant. But when she's making love, she's so distant. It's as if she's not completely there. I think she's thinking about how best to write about what's happening," Zoey sighed.

"The end is near, I can feel it coming."

"You sounded fine together on the phone," Nora lied, trying to cheer her up. "She must be so jazzed. I would be too, I guess, writing something for Reecie Baldwin."

"Bull! She went up there to be alone, Nore. I even asked her if she wanted me to come up last weekend, just for one night. 'The muse is on my back,' she said, 'It'd be far too distracting.'"

"Well, Reecie, she just probably surprised her and she couldn't get out of it."

"Reecie Baldwin was her very first lover. It was years ago. Still, her very first. And then, on the phone, did you hear?" Nora nodded, embarrassed. "I thought you did. All that bit about Reecie being so emotional and her being impassioned and forgetting how well they work together, and then turning it around. Hitting the fan because you're here. All that flack about us never getting over each other. That's her brilliant talent, beginning to construe her pathway out, her escape route. It's okay. I'll let her have the honor." Nora stared at the ceiling, not daring to look at Zoey. "Do you think she's right, Zoe? Do you think I've never gotten over you? I honestly thought I just wanted your friendship and the ability I know you have to cut through all the crap and make me feel better."

"It's maybe a little of everything." Zoey leaned over and looked down at Nora intently. "Maybe she was right about me, too. When you do come running, I drop everything. You always come first."

Nora lifted her hand to touch Zoey's face. She traced her jaw line with a finger. "I kinda like your jaw line, too," she whispered.

Zoey brushed the hair back from Nora's face. "Whatever the reason, I'm just glad I can help, Nore. Feel better now, honey?"

"I guess. I just don't know what to do about Alison or Brie."

"Do you know what you want, Nore?"

"Maybe. I don't know. Do you?"

The question was off the wall and it surprised Zoey.

She asked that question on a daily basis, but nobody ever asked it of her. She visibly blanched, her head involuntarily jerking back as though slapped in the face.

That face was very close to Nora's, her huge blue eyes, reflecting the flames from the fire, dazzled Nora.

They searched Nora's face for a long moment. "Clueless is right," Zoey finally whispered, her fingers playing with Nora's hair. "You are just clueless, honey. I've been hitting on you myself for the last couple of minutes and you never even noticed."

"There's the therapist again," Nora erupted. "My God, Zoey! You'll do anything to make a point. You never quite get out from behind your desk, do you? That was below the belt. Pretending, and testing me like that. Maybe if it had been for real. Maybe if you stopped hiding behind your desk and really hit on me I would notice! So, your test is invalid, incorrect independent variables."

"Leading to a faulty conclusion." Zoey laughed. "You've studied just enough psychology to be dangerous. You're right, though. I do try to retreat from my feelings and hide behind my desk."

"You use that desk like a God damn shield. It keeps you from feeling vulnerable."

"I do, but not this time. I meant it for real. I was hitting on you."

"Oh yeah, right! I know you too well to ever believe that. You with all your boundaries and rules and principles and lines that can't be crossed."

"I think I was. I didn't meant to," Zoey sighed, "I'm sorry."

"I'm sorry, too. Sorry for what I said about you and your desk. Even though I think being a therapist has messed with your head on occasion, I think you're pretty well integrated. I just want your friendship I tell myself, but you notice that I glom onto all the freebies, too. I'll take the whole package. Thanks for tonight. I hope you don't feel used. I know you really hate it when people try to use you. I really needed a friend tonight, but I'm glad the pro was there, too."

"She wasn't there, not really. If I had behaved professionally, I would have left dinner after the salad. I never would have invited you in. Never would have opened more wine. Tonight was me at my most unprofessional."

"Then thanks for that, for letting me in. I feel so much better about us. As painful as all that was to hear, at least I was able to listen. Now maybe someday I can understand what happened to us. And even though we aren't together, at least I know you're there for me. That we're still close, that we can still talk. We haven't really talked like this since...since..."

"Try never, Nore. We've never talked like this."

They stared at each other for a long time. "I'm really different now," Nora offered. "Neat as a pin, too tired every night to have people over and I talk now."

Zoey stood up. "I'm finding that out," she smiled, hands on her hips.

Nora grasped Zoey's hands. "I bet we could make it work, Zoe. You know we love each other," she whispered, embarrassed and shy.

"Maybe so, honey. But maybe it's just the vodka and the wine and you by the firelight looking so hauntingly beautiful. For now, I'm going to take my virtuous, honorable, principled body to bed."

She turned off the light, rearranged the sofa pillows, tidied up and locked up. Then she watched from the doorway as Nora slipped out of her sweats and between the sheets in the guest room.

"I guess maybe you never do get over your very first lover," Nora said wistfully to her very first lover. She got the spotlight grin in return...sudden and blinding.

8

"Nore! Nora! Goddess of Honor!" Zoey called out from the kitchen. She was referring to the Greek name, 'Honora' – of which Nora is a diminutive – and which means 'Honorable.' "Uppy up up, Nora!" Now at the door to the guest room, Zoey continued her cheery assault on Nora's dormant state.

Groggy and disoriented, Nora sat up and looked around. She yawned, stretched and flicked her hair behind her ears. "Christ! I was just comatose! I don't know when I've been in such a deep sleep."

"Coffee's ready in the kitchen. I need to get to the seminar. I'm opening this morning. You can either slip into some clothes, drive me over and drop me off, or just give me your car keys, roll over and go back to sleep."

"What time will you be done?"

"Eleven thirty. What do you have going this morning?"

"My ten o'clock canceled, canceled for good. He went home to mom and dad and will continue therapy there. Most of my day was tied up around him: presenting condition, evaluation, therapeutical schedule, prognoses." Nora shrugged and yawned again. "I wish I could sleep until eleven thirty but I better not. I'll drop you off."

She heaved herself out of bed and into her sweats like a fireman answering the bell. She stumbled into the john and examined herself in the mirror. "Gross! I look like shit."

"What about me?" Zoey appeared with a mug of coffee that she left on the bathroom sink. "Not only do I look like shit, I feel like it too. Whatever possessed me last night? I never do that! Never! And knowing I have to speak this morning, why on earth?"

"What's the topic?" Nora splashed cold water on her face and grabbed for a towel.

"Conquering self-sabotage through goal setting, behavior modification and disciplinary guidelines," Zoey recited into the mirror.

Nora socked her on the arm and they both laughed all the way to the car. Once in the car the conversation turned serious. "I need a Kings X on last night, Nore. A serious Kings X on everything and anything I might have said." Zoey sounded contrite yet casual as she continued. "I haven't had that much to drink since college."

"Probably true," Nora thought.

"Just promise you forgive me for anything I might have done or said last night, that I don't remember this morning."

"Probably not totally true," Nora thought. "You were fine, Zoe. I was distraught and you were there for me. That's the important thing."

"Then that's what's important to me, too. We'll both disregard the details," Zoey grinned that grin. "Whatever they were," she added the outright fib looking Nora right in the eye.

"This is as good a place as any," Zoey indicated a small parking lot and Nora pulled in. "Pick me up here at eleven thirty. Oh, I almost forgot, here's my key."

"Oh, right," Nora muttered. "See ya." She put the car in gear and hurried off, anxious to leave Zoey before she started to blush. She didn't want Zoey, or anyone else for that matter, to see her embarrassment, or to discover that she still had a key to Zoey's front door. That four years, and four zillion traumas later, that key was still on her key ring.

Zoey would make something big out of that, all right. No doubt something about moving on. And, Nora supposed she would make a solid argument. Nora, herself, preferred to chalk it up to sloth. And the usual procrastination that seemed to govern her day to day existence. Stopped at a signal, she looked down at her key ring with renewed interest. Besides her ignition key, car door key and the keys to Gabriella's house and garage, she had keys to her office, her parents' house, Zoey's, Char and Jamie's, where she stayed after Zoey's and before Gabriella's and a couple of keys for her old Honda, plus the newest addition, Sybil's condo.

Nora let herself into Zoey's front door, and slipped the key she had just given her onto her key ring. The thought crossed her mind that she ought to take the time, right then to get rid of the irrelevant keys. But she yawned again and checked her watch. It was almost eight-thirty. Just another hour of sleep would help her deal, Nora thought, as she pulled the bed covers over her, sweats and all.

As it turned out, Nora barely woke up in time to shower, dress and pick up Zoey. Out of the shower with her hair still damp, Nora went in search of her clothes from the night before. She hadn't worn a bra and had turned her underwear inside out, an old trick from high school overnights. Now, getting dressed in Zoey's room, she found herself confronted with Zoey's unmade bed. Last night, properly made up, it had seemed like all of the rest of the décor, just furniture. But now, disheveled and revealing all of itself, it seemed so intimate. Intimate and personal. Nora felt like she was intruding. A part of her wanted to run out of the room. Another part could not drag itself away. Her hand touched the pillow.

There was still an impression from where Zoey's head had been. Nora withdrew her hand as though that pillow was red hot. Indeed, she could get burned here, Nora realized as she backed away from the bed.

She locked the front door with her old key, just to see if it still worked. It did, and she arrived to pick up Zoey just as Zoey, both hands clutching a large wad of napkins, was making her way down the path to the parking lot.

"I hope that's something to eat," Nora began.

Zoey looked at Nora's still wet hair and laughed out loud as she got in the car. "I knew it! I knew you'd go back to bed and get up barely in time to get here. I also knew you'd be starving when you arrived." Zoey uncovered and spread out a couple of paper plates full of assorted sandwiches, little bags of chips and some cookies.

"Great, we can have a car-nick." Nora scarfed down a cookie.

"And then can you take me to get my car? It should be ready by noon."

"Sure. Can we go by Gabriella's first? I have to pick up my mail and get some things. I want to get there and leave before one, in case she comes home."

"Ooh, I don't like this," Zoey shook her head as she followed Nora inside. "It feels like breaking and entering."

"It does to me, too." Nora turned in a complete circle. "It feels so wrong, so empty. It sure isn't home anymore," she added, tears in her eyes.

"Come on. Get your rear in gear and let's get out of here."

They went from the entry through the dining area and into the kitchen. "I need to get my allergy medicine," Nora explained. Zoey paid special attention to the elaborate display of pots, pans and utensils hanging from the two ceiling racks and the continuous wire rack that belted the kitchen walls. Every conceivable mixing, measuring, preparing or cooking device was represented at the ready. Nora opened a walk-in pantry and Zoey's eyes popped out at the contents. Not that she would ever want all that stuff. Gabriella and Nora could have thrown together a last minute feast for forty, no problem.

"Who's the cook?" Zoey couldn't help but ask.

"Both of us, I guess. Me, mostly, but, well, we remodeled the kitchen, you know, and Brie has a client. A cookbook co-author who does a lot of Provencal stuff, lots of magazine spreads, and he persuaded a friend of his to design our remodel. We let them photograph the whole thing when we were finished, so he ended up purchasing all the staples and spices. The condiments, I think he said."

Nora peeked out of the pantry. "He even furnished our refrigerator. Seven hundred and forty two bucks just to fill the door and the shelves. I almost croaked, but Brie was more realistic. 'What's the point of having it all if you don't have it all,' she told me." Nora dumped various plastic bottles into a large garbage bag. Then she turned off all the kitchen lights and left the room.

They proceeded through the living room, up the stairs and down a long hallway with two bedrooms on their right and a large bathroom across the hall from them. Nora went briefly into the bathroom and got some conditioner, shampoo and lotion, as well as a hairdryer. "I don't want to abscond with any of our open bottles; that would piss Brie off." Nora dumped them all into the plastic bag, and they continued down the hall to the master bedroom.

Nora pulled another large plastic bag from under an arm, gave it a resounding shake, and began to fill it with underwear, hose, socks, pajamas, robes, sweats and other clothes.

The bed was unmade in this room, too. Personal and revealing, it screamed at both of them. The top sheet was completely un-tucked and twisted into a loose rope. Pillows were everywhere, except where they should have been. That is, somewhere near the headboard. The quilt, which also served as a bedspread, was slung against the headboard, part of it hanging over the top.

While Zoey was fascinated by this manifestation of potential dementia, and the volumes the bed spoke of its recent occupant, Nora was physically and emotionally so profoundly affected, that it made her nauseous.

"How about this stuff?" Zoey pointed to more casual clothes hanging in the closet. Her real motive was to distract Nora, to take her mind off the distressing condition of the surroundings and focus her once again on their reason for being there.

"I don't have room for any more," Nora grunted, as she fastened the ties on the two bags. "This is all I can fit in the back seat."

Zoey frowned at her. "What are you talking about? You could stack these two, maybe three high."

"Not and still see out the windows."

"Well, just for an hour or two, you could explain if you did get stopped, although I doubt seriously that you will, it's only till you unload."

Nora broke in, "That's the point, Zoe. I don't know when I will unload. Sybil doesn't have a lot of space. I have to prioritize. Stuff I don't have room for I'll just leave in the car, get it out when I need it."

Zoey nodded. "Well, in that case, shouldn't you start with your better clothes? You don't want them wadded up in your car."

"Exactly! But I don't have anything to put them in. I'm not putting them in plastic bags."

"How about your luggage? We could put it in the trunk."

"The trunk is full, Zoey. That's where my luggage is."

"Well, great. Let's go get it. We can pack quite a bit in it."

"Zoe," Nora said slowly, "the luggage is full already."

"Then you need to unpack it at Sybil's and bring it back here. It's by far the most effective way to transport the good stuff," Zoey advised.

"Zoe, I can't. I can't unpack it at Sybil's. There isn't anywhere to put it. I just have to live out of my car for the time being."

Zoey wrinkled her nose as though she smelled something rank. "I have those hanging bags in the garage. They're mothproof and mostly empty since you...since I live alone. You're welcome to them. Maybe just put them in Sybil's garage if they won't fit anywhere else."

"Thanks. That's a really good idea. I was thinking I'd rather leave everything here than see it get beaten up." Nora sighed, "But then accessing it would be a problem. The clothes would be okay, but I would probably get beaten up trying to get them."

The conviction with which this was said was not lost on Zoey. She glanced hastily at her watch. "It's twelve forty five. I would really hate to get caught here with you," she whispered. Her eyes zeroed in on the king-size bedlam bed.

Hearts pounding like the voyeurs they felt akin to, they ran, carrying their plastic bags, out to the car. Nora started the engine. "Shit!" she looked at Zoey. "I forgot my E-mail, the answering machine and my mail."

"Well, make it snappy. I'm staying right here." Zoey rolled down the window and took a deep breath.

9

Arriving at the Jaguar dealer's forty minutes later, it was Nora's turn to wait in the car. Digging out her wallet and checkbook, Zoey smiled cheerily at the cashier and handed her the estimate. The girl was new on the job, Zoey was sure, because she knew all of the regulars. Was, in fact, one of them, she grimaced ruefully. The new girl called Zig, the service department manager. Zoey had only to look to her left to see him pick up the phone in his office, across the driveway. He waved then to Zoey: "Sorry," he mouthed, shrugging his shoulders.

Zoey's attention returned to the cashier. "They had to get an ignition switch from downtown. It just got here an hour ago and they're still working on it. Zig says it will be a couple of hours."

Zoey nodded grimly and without a word, returned to Nora. "It'll be a couple more hours, about three thirty. You might as well dump me at home and go on about your business. I can take a cab back here."

"Don't be silly. If you want to tag along, I'll bring you back. I don't have that much of anything to do. I was just going to Sybil's to try to get organized. You can help me."

"Why not!" Zoey tried to overcome her feelings of helplessness and betrayal. After all, it was only a car. Better to be with Nora than to sit at home, seething. "Do you like your car, Nore?"

"What's not to like? I loved my Honda. This is just a bigger, better Honda," she patted the Acura's dash. At the same time, she thought, "Here comes Zoey's hate/love diatribe about her car."

Sure enough, Zoey slouched in her seat. "I must have some intrinsic motivation for driving that car. Why else would I put up with this? I am a reasonably well-ordered person with a reasonably well-ordered life. That car is my one and only constant aggravation. It's so simple, really so simple, what would I tell me to do about it!"

"You wouldn't tell you anything. You're not in the business of telling people anything. You might point out that sometimes people put up with all kinds of annoyances and aggravation because the pay off is worth it to them."

"Yeah, right. But what kind of pay off are we talking here? It's certainly not prestige. Everyone who knows me feels sorry for me and thinks I'm nuts!" Zoey exploded.

"It's starting to heat up outside; want me to turn on the air?"

"Oh, sure! Great. Show off for me. I haven't had air conditioning for what, three years?"

Nora flipped it on, full blast. Anything to cool her down a little. Zoey could really go off about her car and Nora didn't want to hear it for the next two hours. "Maybe we should go in the pool," she offered.

"Sybil has a pool? Did I know that?"

"Probably not. You'd have to look out the kitchen or bedroom windows to see it."

Zoey was surprised when Nora suddenly wheeled the Acura around, hit an automatic garage opener on the visor and began to back into a garage. The car stopped and they both got out.

"It's nice of Sybil to let you park in the garage."

"Well, I don't park here. Just need to pass through." Nora smiled and opened a door on the back wall of the garage. "That leads to the stairs and Sybil's condo. This leads to my digs." Nora led the way into a large room. It had a private bath, a sofa that made into a bed, a microwave, two built in burners and a small refrigerator in the wet bar. Best of all, draperies opened to expose sliding glass doors out to a private patio and a not-so private community pool.

Nora surveyed the scene. "I can do laps; maybe get my bod in shape."

"Oh, yeah. It needs that all right," Zoey thought as she watched Nora pull off her blouse and replace it with a bikini bra that had been tossed on the bed.

"Christ! I'm hot. You want to change?"

"Not right now, maybe later. Let's see what you plan to do here."

"Well," Nora looked around bleakly. "There really isn't a closet." She pointed to a wall of shelves and cupboards. "These are really for books and games. Not very deep; all my medicines, vitamins and stuff has to go here. My underwear can go in the bathroom under the sink and the rest, the suitcases and plastic bags I'll either leave on the floor or in the car."

"We could construct a dressing area here, next to the bathroom with those hanging bags from my garage." Zoey's face brightened with excitement.

"We could. That would be great. Except I didn't want to make such a big statement, have my presence be so obvious, and permanent looking."

Zoey looked at her curiously, so Nora continued. "Sybil couldn't have been more gracious. She offered me her guest room and that's where I slept the first couple of nights, but then, well, it was so awkward," Nora began to blush. "The second morning I was here there was this guy, Clyde, in the kitchen fixing breakfast in his robe. He's a salesman. Not around all the time, and Sybil has introduced him to everyone as her cousin. She lives in fear that someone might find out. She would be so mortified!"

"The woman is so phobic!" Zoey shook her head and made her clucking sound. "Talk about prejudiced! God forbid she should be seen with a man."

"Well, that's why I moved downstairs," Nora confided. "I figured I was enough of a burden on Sybil, just being here. She didn't need me to take up residence in her guest room when Clyde was supposed to already be there. Besides, I wanted to give them some privacy. That's why I don't go up the steps and in the front door. I'd be up there with them and have to go down the stairs to the garage. It's the only way to get here. So, Sybil gave me her extra opener. It works out fine."

"Except that Sybil always knows exactly when you come and go."

"Right! And she and Clyde can't go out in back without going through here. See, that's what I meant about making a statement. I don't want them to feel like they are intruding on me when they just want to go outside."

"Hmmmm!" Zoey grunted. "I guess it's best to leave your stuff in the car after all," she thought aloud. "At least until you figure out how long you'll be here."

Nora nodded agreement. "In the beginning, you know, it didn't seem so bad. I thought a week, maybe two, then I'd be back with Gabriella. But now, that doesn't seem to be a possibility at all."

"No." Zoey shook her head.

"Brie won't take me back and even…"

Zoey waited. "Even?" she repeated, encouraging.

"Even if she would I…"

Zoey waited again, finally confronting her. Hands beckoning Nora, she willed it out of her. "I…I can't go there," Nora finally muttered.

Zoey slapped her on the back, kissed her on the cheek and exuberantly yelled, "Yahoo!" Then she watched Nora carefully as she picked up her blouse and absently put it down again.

"I can't, Zoe. I mean it. I really can't go back!" It had just dawned on Nora.

"And doesn't it feel good to know that, Nore? To own that somewhere deep inside?"

"It feels better not to be confused, if that's what you mean. But it feels bad, too."

"Well, sure. It's an ending and there's still all that pain…"

"No!" Nora interrupted. "I mean, it feels bad, Zoey, to feel good about it." The suddenness of the truth hit them both like a ton of bricks. Nora began to cry and Zoey wanted to hold her in her arms. Instead she handed her a tissue.

"Come on, time to take me back to get my car."

Nora had hit the garage door opener and they were just pulling out of the driveway, when the garage door, about half way down, started to go back up again. "What the hell…" but before Nora could finish the sentence or jab the opener again, Sybil came driving up in her SUV.

"Well, hi. Glad I caught you! Just came home to go in the pool," she said, still behind the wheel. "I see you had the same idea," she laughed, pointing at Nora's bathing suit bra.

"Well, I had good intentions, maybe later. Sybil, you know Zoey, of course."

"Zoey? Oh, my God! Zoey! I didn't even see you there!" Sybil opened the car door and climbed down. "I'm up so high in that thing, and you're backed in so weird."

"Well, I was going to unload some stuff."

"Great! Now that I'm here, I can help." Sybil started to open the rear door behind Nora.

"That's okay, Syb. I, uh, decided not to. I have to take Zoey to get her car."

"Oh." Sybil leaned into the car. "Good to see you again, Zoey. Come back later. We can go in the pool."

"Thanks! I'm glad to see you again. I have to take a rain check on the pool, though. Nora just brought me over to see where she was staying. Thanks for letting her stay here. It's really nice of you."

They were out of the driveway and half way down the block before they both spoke at once. Zoey let go with an all-purpose, "Shit!"

But Nora was more verbose. "I am so fucked! So absolutely, totally frigging, fracking, fucked! This will be all over. Brie will find out before sundown."

"But Nore, remember? You can't go back, remember? Just a few minutes ago?"

"Of course I remember. But I want it to be my idea," Nora grumbled. "You didn't help matters thanking her like that."

"I what?"

"You thanked her Zoe."

"I certainly did not!"

"Yes, you did. You said, 'Thanks for letting her stay here.'"

"Well, I just meant, you know, it was nice of her. I felt like I should tell her I thought so, but not like I had any interest, certainly."

"That's not how it came out. It was very proprietary; like she was caring for something that belonged to you."

"Oh, Damn!" Zoey groaned. "Oh, God, I'm so sorry. You know I didn't mean anything. I was just making conversation. Babbling really. You know how I do that when I'm flustered."

"I know that. I was just telling you it doesn't fucking help!"

10

"Please don't think I'm paranoid, but would you wait out in front until I drive by? I'll give you the 'all clear' honk, and then you can leave. I just don't want to be stuck there if it isn't ready."

"No problem! I have nothing much to do, anyway. Where are you going?"

"I'm just going home. I need to go to the market first, pick up some frozen dinners. Then I'll go home and have one. I'm beat. Still have a headache. I'm still paying for last night. What about you?"

"I guess I'll go back to Sybil's. Maybe go in the pool. Make nice to her and try to diffuse the fact that we were together."

"God! Is it really such a big deal?"

"Not for you, Zoe. But, well, in our exclusive little group, yeah, it is. Endless speculation and gossip, it's what they feed on, live for."

"Well, that's patently ridiculous. I certainly have no intention of explaining where I go or who I'm with when I go there. It's nobody's business." Zoey got out of the car and slammed the door.

She knows better than that, thought Nora, watching her walk into the service department office. She knows very well that she's as fucked as I am, maybe more. After all, she's the one in a committed relationship, not me. Nora slid down in her seat, waiting as promised.

She waited and waited. She saw Zoey leave the service department and go across the way to the cashier's office. Then, after a while, she came out and started walking away from the street, and Nora. Then Nora saw Zig come out of his office and go off in the general direction Zoey had taken. It was taking too long, and Nora knew something must be wrong. She also knew that the longer it took, the more wrong the something must be. Therefore

59

it was with both relief and trepidation that Nora saw Zoey reappear. "Shit!" she said to herself. Then, about thirty seconds later, she repeated it to Zoey. "Shit! Now what!"

"You aren't going to believe it." Zoey, thoroughly beaten down, opened the car door and fell into the front seat. "I was so happy! It was almost two hundred dollars more than the quote, but I didn't care. In replacing the ignition switch, they ran into something else." Zoey waved a hand in the air. "I honestly didn't care how much it cost. I went out to the lot and there she was. They had washed her, and she was so beautiful. I got in, she started right up, the engine just purred. I put it in reverse stepped on the accelerator, and she coughed once and died. Then, when I tried to start her again, the starter just whined and whined and the engine wouldn't turn over."

"I just lost it, started beating my fists against the dash and the steering wheel. Someone went to get Zig and they helped me into the waiting room and gave me some water and then Zig came in. 'Soeee,' he said, he pronounces his Z's like S's and his S's like Z's. Soeee, I am zo zorry. Thiz iz zo unfortunate. You zee, Soeee, now I am afraid that the fuel pump needz to be replaced. Zometimes when we redo the ignition, then the fuel pump, it doesn't rezpond. It waz only a matter of time before you would need a new one." Zoey was forlorn looking, but her imitation was so perfect, Nora had to laugh.

"You're right to laugh Nore. It's only a car. I simply have to get a grip. It's only one more day. He said Saturday before noon. Tomorrow is the last day of the seminar but my duties are really over, until Monday when I need to report on the seminar to regional council. Maybe I can use lack of transportation as an excuse to get out of going."

Nora made a face and shook her head, but she let Zoey run on until she was out of gas. "There's really no reason I need to go except that I'm on the welcoming committee. I could say I was sick, or, oh, hell, take me home, would you, Nore?"

"What about food? I thought you said you needed to go to the market. Do you have anything at all to eat?"

"Not a thing. But that's okay. I'm not hungry."

"But Zoe, you will be later!"

"That's okay Nora. I don't want to impose on you any more than I already have. I've practically ruined your whole day."

Nora pulled the car over to the side of the road. "Zoey it isn't your fault. Big deal! Your car wasn't ready. Now you're here and I'm here and neither one of us has anything pressing. You need food. Let's go to the market and stock up. It's the perfect time with me to help you unload."

Zoey grinned her spotlight grin. "You're on! You maybe be sorry you volunteered for this. I've been needing to do this for months. Oh, Polly will be so happy!"

"How is Polly? She still come every Friday?"

"Yep, she's fine, except when her arthritis kicks up. Usually during baseball season, then she has to take a little longer lunch..."

"...depending on who's on the tube," Nora finished for her.

"I could care less, really. She always stays as late as she needs to, to clean the whole place. I'm never home anyway. What's the difference?"

It was close to six o'clock when they pulled into Zoey's driveway. Since the car was full before they went shopping, it was now really stuffed. Nora had to get out and open the passenger side front door, and remove several grocery bags in order to uncover Zoey enough to allow her to climb out of the car. Bags literally filled the back seat all the way to the headliner. The trunk, too, had market bags wedged and mounded all around, over and under Nora's luggage.

They had made seven trips a piece into Zoey's kitchen and back out to the car, when breathless, they faced each other across the back seat.

"Just these four, I guess," Nora wiped her forehead with the back of her hand. "Wait! Where's my other plastic bag like this?" she pointed to one she had brought from Gabriella's.

"Oh, shit!" Zoey sagged against the door. "I must have taken it in by mistake. Sorry. we'll find it when I put away."

They emptied the rest of the back seat, Nora locked her car and they trucked everything into Zoey's kitchen.

"Thanks, Nore. Above and beyond the call of duty. I'll buy you dinner!"

"Thanks but no thanks. I don't see how you can eat this stuff." Nora stacked several frozen dinners into the freezer. "Save those puppies for later. I'm fixing dinner tonight, as long as I'm here anyway. Didn't you see the fresh swordfish I got? That was odd, running into Roxanne at the checkout stand, wasn't it! I mean, she looked like she'd seen a ghost. And then she was so short, almost rude. All she said was, 'Well, hello Nora!' And then while you were writing your check, she just stared at you with her mouth open."

"She did? Well, she probably didn't know you were with me. I had already seen her in drugs and feminine supplies. I think you were in dairy and then the fish. We chatted, but it was a little awkward. She wondered why I didn't return to the afternoon session of the seminar. I think she was a little out of joint. She was one of the discussion leaders. I told her I had a patient, and then some personal errands."

"And then she sees me, with a whole cart full of wine, the flowers, the fish and the candles. She was probably about to say, 'Did you see Zoey? She's here too,' when you made the scene."Zoey stopped emptying bags onto the counter and pointed at Nora, "Then you unloaded both of the carts and I," she tapped her chest, "paid for it all."

"And Roxanne damn near fainted," Nora began to laugh. "It is really so stupid. Now she'll think we're together for sure. I mean who would go to the market with someone unless they…"

"Who indeed," Zoey declared. "Well, I for one, could care less what any of them think. Here, put these in the guest bath," she indicated a bag of supplies.

While Nora was doing that the phone rang. She could hear Zoey answer it, hear the happy recognition. "Hi, honey! Just fine! Putting away some groceries."

Nora finished stowing stuff under the bathroom sink and, glancing into the guest room, she noticed that she had forgotten to make the bed. Horrified, she rushed to complete the task before Zoey saw it. It's a good thing I came back here. How embarrassing it would have been if Zoey had seen this, she thought to herself. At the same time, she could hear Zoey's voice, rising in volume.

"I just told you, K. She took me to get my car! We went by Gabriella's on the way!"

Nora gave the spread one last smooth and returned to the kitchen in time to hear Zoey say, "Well, I don't give a damn what Gabriella said or didn't say. Or what Sybil told her. I'm telling you what happened. Now, do you want to hear what I have to say or not?"

Nora washed and drained some lettuce, and put some paper towels in the refrigerator vegetable drawers. Then she put some paper napkins in the napkin holder on the bar. Zoey had really been out of everything.

"I'm sorry to hear you say that, and I'm sorry that's how you feel, K. But you're blowing this entire thing out of proportion. Nora picked me up at the seminar and took me to get my car. We stopped at Gabriella's to get a few things. My car wasn't ready and we had two hours to kill. Not enough time to do much of anything, but too much time to just sit at the car dealership, so Nora took me over to Sybil's to show me where she was staying. I told her

I'd help her get organized. Sybil, you know Sybil Sharpwhite. She's the talk show Director at KWSS. Remember that Herbie Whatshisname that had you on to plug your book? Yes, that Sybil. So we went over there for a bit and were just leaving when Sybil arrived. We exchanged a quick hello and goodbye and then Nora took me back to get my car."

Nora put a bottle of wine in the refrigerator, and then began putting bottles in the wine rack, under the bar. On second thought, she put a couple more bottles in the refrigerator. Then she started putting away the cans and boxes of food. This was not too difficult as everything was exactly as it had been before, when this was her own kitchen. The thought made her smile, and she reached up into the high cupboard over the burners and the exhaust fan. Still there, she thought triumphantly as she retrieved a bag containing her small stash of candles and cake decorations. She had liked to surprise Zoey with special occasion cakes and didn't want Zoey to find the decorations ahead of time so she hid them.

What a kid! she thought, as she peaked in the bag. What she saw in there made her eyes sting and fill with tears. Sweet, sweet innocence, a belief in one true love. A one and only, forever and ever.

Still holding the phone with one hand, Zoey looked at her curiously and held out her other hand. Nora gave her the bag. Zoey surveyed the contents and then closed her eyes.

Nora knew she was no longer listening to Kirsten, but remembering some long ago surprise, real or feigned. A moment in the history shared by the two of them, a moment of tenderness and adoration freely given and accepted without hesitation, doubt or mistrust. A moment that never would, never could, come again.

Zoey opened her eyes and motioned with her hands for Nora to open some wine and pour them a glass. "Good. Good honey, I'm relieved, too. No, I knew that. Just glad you feel better about it. Okay, and you do the same. I love you too. Goodnight." Zoey let the receiver drop onto the phone on the counter.

"Christ! Gabriella called her, supposedly about her agent's contract. But really, to let her know that she came home for lunch and saw you and I there. She waited in her car until we left so she wouldn't have to confront us together. Kirsten was steamed, really steamed, but once I explained, once she understood, she was all right with it."

"Gabriella has funny issues sometimes. She was probably upset that you were there."

"And that I saw her bed," Zoey nodded, thinking about it. "If that was my bed, I would have been humiliated to have anyone see it."

Nora was just pouring their wine when her cell phone rang. Surprised, she took it out of her purse, rolled her eyes to the ceiling, answered, and put it on speakerphone to share with Zoey.

"Hi, Nora," came Sybil's voice. "Sorry to bother you. I know you're at Zoey's."

"No problem, Sybil. We're just putting away groceries.'

"So I heard. Roxanne said you were stocking up for a storm. Two whole carts full."

"And here comes the storm," Zoey muttered under her breath.

"Yeah, Zoey's car wasn't ready. We had some time to kill. And Zoey was really out of everything. She was glad to have the help."

"I'm sure she was! You can come with me anytime, Nora. But that isn't why I called. You know I could care less about anyone's personal business, but Gabriella called and I told her you weren't here. She wanted to know if you had been here and I said yes, that you had. I never would have mentioned Zoey, never, but she asked specifically. What could I say? I mean, I wasn't going to just lie outright, and you never said not to tell."

"Hey! That's fine, really, Sybil. You were just fine. Brie knows I was with Zoey last night. We had dinner together. I took her to get her car; no big deal."

"As long as you're not angry with me, as long as you trust me. That's all I care about."

"Of course I'm not angry. And of course I trust you," Nora rolled her eyes to the ceiling again.

"Great! Will I be seeing you later then or are you staying over at Zoey's?" Sybil took a triumphant breath before adding the zinger, "Again."

Nora gave Zoey a look. "You know, I have a lot to do Syb. I'm not sure yet. Don't count on me; I'll call you if I'm coming." Nora flipped the cover down on the cell phone. "I wonder if there's any way I can sneak in to Sybil's. I just can't handle her any more tonight."

"I totally sympathize." Zoey took a large swallow of wine. "The woman drives me up the wall. She's so shrill."

Zoey gathered up the cleaning supplies on the counter and carried them to the laundry room.

Nora regarded the kitchen; orderly and tidy once again. "Where's my bag? The one you brought in by mistake?"

"Oh, shampoo? Conditioner?" Nora nodded. "I threw all the bathroom stuff in it. That's the one I gave you to put in the guest bath."

"Never mind," Nora held Zoey by the arm, "don't bother about it now. Let's just have our wine and relax. What a day!"

11

Zoey settled on a stool at the bar. "Nothing went right all day!"

"Well it wasn't that bad. Only your car."

"And the fact that I accomplished nothing that I had planned to accomplish."

"So we went to the market instead. That was a major accomplishment."

"And you admitted to yourself that you aren't going back to Gabriella, ever. That was big Nora. I'm proud of you."

"Yeah, you're right. It feels good, even though it still feels bad to feel so good about it. I have to admit, it is easier to feel better about it after she called Sybil like that."

At that moment Nora's cell phone rang again. She picked it up and looked at it. "Speaking of the devil," she groaned. "Hi Sybil."

"I'm sorry. I really am, Nora. But I thought I ought to let you know. Right after we talked, that friend of Zoey's called, that writer, Chris something."

"Kirsten?" Nora's surprised expletive got Zoey's attention. Eyes wide, they both stared at Nora's cell phone.

"She wanted to know if you were here or if I knew where you were. I said 'No' to both, of course. I guess Gabriella called her. 'But she is staying there with you,' Chris said. 'I mean her clothes and things are already there, not at Gabriella's anymore?' And, I thought that she was thinking it was sort of mean of you, or shallow, you know, clearing everything out of Gabriella's so quickly, like you had decided the relationship was over without even trying to fix it. I guess I was a little defensive. A little protective of you. Anyway, I told Chris that when I saw you, you still had a lot of your things in your car and I wasn't sure if you were going to move more in here or not. That you had said you were, but then decided not to, and that you and Zoey went to get her car. I did tell her that, but that's all. I swear! That's all I said."

"And," Nora prompted without wanting to hear the reply.

"And she went berserk, just crazy, screaming and crying. I couldn't understand what she was yelling about. Something about 'screw the second act' and 'the finale has come.' Anyway, I thought I'd better tell you that she'd be early."

"Early for what? What are you talking about Syb?"

"Just that, you know, she was coming tomorrow…driving down. Gabriella told me. They have a meeting scheduled for three."

"You're sure?" Zoey and Nora were both puzzled. "Zoey talked to her earlier, and Kirsten never mentioned it."

"Oh, no! Oh, God! I hope I didn't blow it. She was probably going to surprise Zoey. Listen, Nora, maybe you'd better not tell her. Just clear out. Let them be alone together. Chris will probably be there in a couple of hours."

"Maybe I'll do that Sybil, and thanks for filling me in."

Nora hung up and the two of them stared at each other.

"Thank God for Sybil." Zoey's smile was sheepish. "What was it I was just saying about her?"

"I think you said she was shrill."

"Right, but I meant that in the best sense of the word." Zoey finished her glass of wine, stood up and put it in the dishwasher. "I don't know about you, but I am not the least inclined to wait here for the tempest to arrive," she added in a huff as she walked past Nora.

"Where are you going to go? And how are you planning to get there?"

Nora grinned as Zoey kicked the laundry room door shut in utter frustration. "Why do I want to leave? It's my house! Why do I feel guilty? I haven't done anything wrong. Actually, the funny thing is, I was thinking about surprising Kirsten this weekend. My sister invited some friends up to the lake next weekend. She almost never goes, doesn't know how things work. I thought I'd run up there sometime this weekend and make sure everything is ship shape, turn on the water and the propane. Nobody's been there for months, probably. Then, I thought, well, I'd be about half way to Kirsten's. Maybe I'd go on up and see her," Zoey rubbed her eyes. "But then I was ambivalent about surprising her. Didn't know what I might find."

"Apparently Kirsten is not bothered by any such ambivalence," Nora grunted. Then she went into the laundry room and returned with an ice chest. She filled it with wine and ice and threw the swordfish on top.

Zoey regarded her without comprehension.

"Come on, let's go right this minute," she told an astounded Zoey. "Get another pair of sweats for me. Everything else I could possible need is already in my car."

"But I can't just up and leave like that! Are you crazy?"

"I don't see why not!"

"Well because I need to make arrangements, tell people where I'm going."

"No, you don't. Why do you? Just once, for once in your life do something on impulse!"

"Okay, but leave the fish here. We'll get there too late to have it tonight."

"Tonight we'll have fast food in the traffic. We'll have the fish tomorrow night."

"Why not?" Zoey grinned that grin.

Thirty minutes later, after some last minute loading and unloading, they were ready to leave. To be on the safe side, they took the sleeping bags and some old towels. But in order to make room for those in the trunk, Nora's largest suitcase, containing some blazers and pantsuits had to be unloaded. Zoey stuck it in her closet where she knew Polly would leave it alone.

After a moment's thought, she pulled the suitcase back out and heaved it up on the bed. "Here, help me hang these up. It'll just take a second. I can't bear to think of these beautiful things all twisted up like this."

"Is it likely to be dusty up there?" Nora asked as she changed into Zoey's sweats from last night.

"Yes, I'd say it is likely to be more than dusty." Zoey picked up Nora's discarded clothes, folded them and put them in the top dresser drawer. "Polly freaks out if you leave clothes laying around."

"Yeah, I remember. What's the point of having her if you have to clean up before she comes." Nora groused from under the guest bathroom sink. After rummaging for a bit, she came up with a large bottle of pills. She sat on the john in Zoey's bathroom and emptied as many as she could into a smaller vial, which she threw into her purse. Then she screwed the lid back on and started to leave the large bottle on the sink. She and Zoey exchanged a look. "Polly," they said in the same breath, and Nora put the bottle in the medicine cabinet.

"Do not let me forget that stuff."

"Impossible! When you can't breathe, you'll remember on your own." They left a bathroom light on, locked up and drove directly to Zoey's ATM machine. Nora wanted to eat while they were still in the city and the traffic, and she didn't want to get on the freeway and then off again.

"Fast food is fine with me. It all tastes the same." Zoey was easy, used to her frozen dinners. "You know something? I'm excited, Nore! Really excited! Just to do something so unexpected, so spur of the moment! It's such a charge."

"It's also a control thing, Zoe. Having some control over your life after an entire day of having none, zero, zilch." Nora was not above the occasional educated observation.

Zoey was appreciative. "That's right on, Nora! Positively right on."

"Some might call it acting out," Nora retorted.

Nora had just finished her burger and was working on some fries when the cell phone rang. Zoey got it out of Nora's purse. "Maybe you shouldn't answer this," she speculated. "Do we want anyone to know where we're going?"

Licking her fingers, Nora thought. "Read me the number. If it's Sybil, I have to take it. I mean, she'll know I'm deliberately not answering it because it's her."

Zoey read her the number. "It's my service. I'll call them back later and get my messages. I need to tell them I won't be in anyway. I don't have any patients tomorrow. Just a staff meeting first thing, then some paperwork at the clinic." Nora thought aloud.

"And all I have is that blasted seminar. Well, I'll just have to think of something."

"But what if Sybil does call?"

"The secret with people like Sybil is to do unto them before they do unto you!" Zoey gathered up their dinner remains and scrunched everything back into the bag. "What I mean is, there must be a way we can use Sybil, with her unique talents, to our best advantage. We need to make her an ally, a trusted friend, you know?"

"I know exactly," Nora grinned and reached for the phone. "Syb? Oh good. You are still there. Listen, can you do me a favor? Zoey had something come up. A house call." Nora looked at Zoey and they nodded together. "She still doesn't have her car, so I'm taking her. We don't know exactly what she's getting into, so could you call Roxanne and ask her to let everyone know at the seminar, in case Zoey doesn't get back in time? Oh, and don't bother to call Gabriella or anything, but if she calls you, if she wonders where I am, just tell her."

"Okay, no problem, Nora. Where are you going?"

"I don't know. Zoey has the directions."

"Well, I'll take care of everything. Don't worry. Talk to you later."

"That's the thing, Syb. I'll call you when I can. I have to turn my phone off right after we hang up. You know some of these cases. If extreme psychosis is involved, a ringing phone could trigger, God knows what! Thanks again Sybil."

"Good luck. Hang in there, you guys. Tell Zoey I'm proud to count her as a friend."

Zoey looked out the window in silence for a while. "I could have done without the last sentence. We're using her shamelessly and she thinks she's my friend."

"Oh, Zoe, come on. It's Sybil, for God's sake! If she gets some big charge out of knowing where we are and thinking we're confiding in her, so what! We've made her day. I bet she's on the phone to Roxanne already."

"I bet she'll call Gabriella first."

"You're probably right and the funny thing is, you don't even know her," Nora chuckled.

Zoey handed Nora the Coke she was holding for her. "Oh, but I do, Nore. Sybil is in my office every day, every God Damn day. She's either there in person as a patient, or in spirit, as one who put the patient there. She's the symbol for, and the perfect example of, the aging single female in our society, gay or straight.

"Unfulfilled, her options narrowing year by year, her world shrinking, she becomes involved with minutia... lives her life through her friends and her friends' friends, throws herself into her work. The only 'juice' in her life comes from the occasional break ups and make ups in her friends' love lives."

"Well, I don't know about you, but life's too short! I'm going to live mine myself with all the juice I can squeeze into it. I refuse to live my life through others."

"Way to go, Nore. I believe you. And I know you mean it, too. But while you refuse to live your life through others, you will still be living it for others. For all the Sybil's of the world."

"Except for times like this when I sneak around," Nora added good-naturedly.

As they left the city behind, the traffic began to lighten up and so did their moods. "This is so perfect! I can just see Kirsten barging in the front door, mad as all hell, and surprise, nobody's there."

"I only wish I was there. Just to see her face."

"Not me. I'll have to face her down eventually, but I intend to wait until her fury melts down to mere venomous indignation. She is impossible to reason with when she's really pissed."

"So is Brie. But she wraps all of her other emotions in guilt. It covers and smothers everything else until finally, that's all you are left with. No matter what you started out thinking you were up against."

Zoey looked at her sharply. "You really are out of that, aren't you?"

"Apparently! I guess I am! I think knowing that she called Sybil and Kirsten, of course she may have had a real reason to call Kirsten, something business related. Still it seems so intrusive."

"What about Kirsten calling Sybil like that? Talk about intrusive. She must really not trust me at all. That gives me the creeps. You know how important trust and honesty are to me."

"If she doesn't trust you to begin with, then you iced that cake tonight."

"Hardly! I wasn't the one calling all around," Zoey protested.

"No, Zoe. You were the one who explained everything to Kirsten. I heard you. You were the soul of patience, explaining in great detail about your car and me. The only thing you left out was that I was still in your kitchen. So, when Kirsten found out from Sybil that I was there and she had just talked to you and you had neglected to mention that, she went ape shit."

"I never said you weren't there, Nora," Zoey was defensive.

"No, but you intimated. You led her to believe that you were alone."

"Not on purpose! I'm not responsible for what Kirsten deduces from a phone conversation!" Zoey snapped. "I don't play those games! You know me better than that!"

Nora had to laugh. "Then who was that who signaled me with sign language to open a bottle of wine and pour us each a glass?"

"Got me!" Zoey laughed, too. "Christ, I can be such a sanctimonious, self-righteous bitch sometimes. How do you stand me? I can hardly stand me myself."

"Well, I don't, of course. I don't have to stand you at all anymore. But, if I did, I mean if we were together, I'd answer that the same way I always did answer it. Because you're *my* sanctimonious, self-righteous bitch of course."Zoey zapped her with that grin. "Tell me the truth. I'm impossible sometimes, I know that. Are you relieved that...that you don't have to stand me?"

"God, Zoey I can't believe you could ask me that. I never found you

72

difficult, ever. I just loved you. Loved everything about you, and I was so in love with you I was honestly unable to criticize or disapprove of any of your behavior."

"Hero worship! Oh, you were so young, so naïve. And I was too stupid to appreciate your unrealistic perception of me when I had it. Of course, now is another story."

"But that's what I mean, Zoey. I don't know if I'm relieved to not put up with you now because I don't have anything to contrast it with. Even when we broke up, I kept going over and over stuff, looking for the bad things. I couldn't even find any then. Roberta said it was because I was blaming myself, trotting out the old self-image, blaming my unworthiness on driving you away. Roberta said if I did anything, it was to set you up on a pedestal, adore you, and not believe you could do anything human, let alone anything outright wrong! She said we all do things that we want to do that turn out not to be in somebody else's best interest. That's just life: romance, dating and life in general."

"Get off at the next ramp: White Lake Boulevard. What else did Roberta say?" Zoey was morbidly fascinated.

Nora got off the highway. "You'll have to tell me when to turn. I don't remember Roberta saying anything else. Just that it was a natural part of life. One time she did bring me a tape that she had recorded from her CD at home...Ella Fitzgerald."

"Really? I love Ella. Singing what?"

Nora shrugged. "Beats me! I can sing it for you, though. I probably played it ten thousand times." With that she pulled over and put the car in park. Then she began quietly, "The devil was in your heart, but heaven was in your eyes the night that you told me those little white lies."

Zoey held her breath. Tears stung her cheeks. Nora went on.

"Who wouldn't believe those lips, whoever could doubt those eyes, the night that you told me..." Nora stopped abruptly, "told me you needed time to decide between Kirsten and me. To decide who was right for you." Nora was barely whispering. "I waited and waited, on pins and needles. I was a wreck Zoe. I couldn't do anything, just waiting for you to decide. Later Roberta told me it was just a little white lie. You were trying to not hurt me so much. Instead, it made it ten times worse. I expected you at any moment, see. And you never did tell me what you decided. And Roberta said you probably forgot...forgot...that was the worst time of my life. For days I obsessed about that. That you forgot...forgot that you left me bleeding to death." Nora's whisper faded and the silence that enveloped them seemed a physical thing. Tears ran down both of their faces as they stared out the windshield of the car, not looking at each other.

"So, see, I honestly don't know if I'm relieved at not having to stand you now or not," Nora smiled through her tears.

"Can you ever forgive me, Nore?" It was Zoey's turn to whisper between sobs.

"I don't think so. I don't think I can, Zoe."

"But will you…will you please try?"

Nora could barely hear her. She grabbed Zoey's hand and gave it a squeeze. "I promise. I will, if I can."

Zoey nodded, passed Nora a tissue and blew her nose. "Turn left up there at the signal and then it's four miles exactly to the fork in the road. Go to the right and look for the big yellow house on the left. Turn left at the first little street past it. We'll be there in fifteen minutes," Zoey added, thank God, to herself. She could not handle much more time in this car.

12

One hour later found Zoey tramping around in front of the cabin and Nora trying to maneuver the car so that its headlights would give Zoey some help.

"You're sure you don't want me to light a flare?"

"God, no! We'd probably set the whole mountain on fire. I can't believe you don't have a flashlight in your glove box, though. I thought I gave you one."

"You did, 1994 I think it was. I also had a Girl Scout one, hung on my belt and banged against my knee. I was so embarrassed when our leader demonstrated how we all needed to remove our flashlights from our belts before attempting to use them."

"Aha!" Zoey called out in triumph. "Here's the elf and froggie pot. Clear over here; stuck in the gnarl of this tree trunk. Now if the key is only…yes!" she held it up for Nora to see. "Why the hell would some idiot stick this way over there," Zoey went on, annoyed.

"Probably because the last idiot here was concerned about three or four feet of snow covering elfie and froggie all up," Nora teased, in baby talk, as she followed Zoey into the cabin. A light switch next to the door turned on a couple of wall fixtures and a large hanging one, descending from the open beamed ceiling.

"Man, that's harsh!" Zoey declared as she went about turning on lamps and turning off the bright fixtures.

Nora grabbed the flashlight on the table right next to the front door, just where Zoey said it would be, and went out to deal with the car. She moved it into the carport where it would be easier to unload through the back door.

Then she proceeded to bring their things in.

Zoey, meanwhile, turned on the water and the propane. They met in the living room.

"There's a bag of ice in the freezer."

"And wood stacked for a fire," Zoey observed. "We're in business."

Nora, carrying the sleeping bags and their duffel bag of clothes, headed in the direction of the two downstairs bedrooms.

"Where are you going with those?"

"Where do you want them?"

Zoey pointed to the stairs.

Nora was startled. "Up there?"

"I don't know. Joan and I always slept up there. I don't think I've ever slept down here," Zoey thought about it.

"Is there a john up there?" Zoey shook her head and Nora made a unilateral decision on the spot. While she dumped everything on one of the beds, Zoey began to build a fire. The very next thing Nora knew she must do was to take an allergy pill.

Then, plopping their purses on the dining table, she got one and went to the kitchen for a glass of water.

This turned out to be easier said than done. When she turned on the tap she was rewarded with an unbearable clanging and banging that brought Zoey on the run.

"It's all right!" she yelled, turning off the spigot. "It's just air in the pipes. Just turn the water on a little at a time and let it run. You don't want to drink any water out of here for ten or fifteen minutes."

Unfazed, Nora left the water off, opened the ice chest, removed the wine bottle with a cork in it, pulled out the cork and washed her pill down with the wine. She held the bottle up to Zoey. "Want some?"

"I guess." Zoey reached for the bottle and took a swig, surprising Nora into gales of laughter. They found some paper cups to more appropriately enjoy their wine and carried them back into the living room, which was now rapidly and alarmingly filling with smoke.

"Shit." Zoey handed Nora her wine, spilling half of it, and ran to the fireplace. Closing her eyes and turning her back to the blaze, she stuck her left arm up the chimney and felt around until she found the damper that opened and closed the flue. "There! That's ever so much easier to do before you light your fire." Zoey brushed her palms together quickly. "Something poor Joan would never think to do," she added, her eyes smarting from the smoke.

"I gotta get out of here," Nora sputtered.

Zoey grabbed two folding chairs from the entry hall and dragged them out the front door onto the porch. "Sit right here! I'll be right back," she assured Nora. Then she ventured back into the now smoke-filled cabin, holding her sweatshirt up over her nose and mouth.

Nora sipped her wine and listened to Zoey opening and closing windows and doors. She was about to start a search party when Zoey finally reappeared. Wrapped in a quilt, with another one in her arms, she also carried a straw bag with a drawstring top.

"I figured we would likely be out here quite some time, so I brought supplies." She set the bag down between them.

"Good plan!" Nora noticed all of the rest of the wine in the bag. "That ought to last us," she snuggled the quilt around her. "Has this ever happened before? The whole place filling with smoke like this?"

"Only just about every time we come up here." Zoey leaned back, laughing, and put her feet up on the railing.

Nora put her feet up too, and had some wine. "It feels good just to sit back and relax. I guess I'm a little tense. Sorry if I got a little uptight earlier."

"Not your fault, Nore, not your fault you did a complete one-eighty ten or twelve times on the road…looking for the big yellow house."

"And not your fault, either Zoe. The look on your face, when you yelled, 'stop the car!' and then you stomped out to that mound of dirt. Walked all around it kicking rocks in disgust. It was really funny."

"Well, I'm glad you, at least, were amused. Who knew, huh? Who knew that the big yellow house would no longer be there. Would be replaced by the big empty lot. I guess it is kind of funny, looking back on it. We kept going back and forth, going farther and slower until I was positive it couldn't be farther down the road. I scrutinized each house. Could this be the yellow house? Painted brown now? It never entered my mind that the house might just be gone. It's so weird. It was more than just a house, you know. It was a landmark. I feel as if the lake itself might as well be gone."

"That was the beginning for me, but still it was funny. What was not funny was crawling around, out in the front here for what seemed like hours looking for the elfie and froggie pot. 'It's always on the porch,' you said, and 'it's always right by the front door.'

Nora was interrupted by Zoey's sudden burst of laughter. "And you…prying up that pre-historical, petrified, animal feces on the walkway,

'What the hell is this stuff?'"

"Filling the cabin with smoke and having to sit out here all night seems a logical conclusion to the evening." Nora refilled their paper cups.

"Yes, arriving and settling in, have historically produced such angst and tension, that when you finally get a chance to sit and relax, the experience is enhanced tenfold." Zoey's spotlight grin lit up the place.

"It's always a hassle?"

"Always! Of course we used to leave at o'dark thirty and get here in the morning. It's easier to deal in the morning with the whole day stretching ahead of you. Note that I did not say easy, only easier. It's never easy."

"Really?" Nora was curious. "Like, well…what happens?"

"Oh, sometimes intruders of one kind or another. Bees inhabited the storage room under the cabin once. Not too many of them came up here, but we had to sleep in the car the first night until the beekeeper could get here and get rid of them. Another time birds got in. Someone forgot to close the flue, hundreds of these little birds, what a nightmare. We shooed out as many as we could but over half of them died. Then we kept finding more all day and Joanie and I wouldn't go to bed. Finally, Dad rigged up some netting to cover our bunk bed to keep the birds off us. I was scared they would still get me on the top bunk, so I slept on the bottom with Joanie. She wet the bed." Zoey laughed thinly, remembering. "It wasn't always wild life that intruded. A couple of times we found evidence that someone had been here. I remember we were scared they might come back, but Mom said not to worry. 'You don't think they would dare come back with your father here. They would be scared to death.' Joanie and I were young enough that we believed that. We still thought he could do anything and everything! Another time some college girls were here, all settled in. But they had made a mistake. They really thought they were in the right cabin, and they were so embarrassed. They weren't a problem. It was only that they had been here a couple of days and they were total pigs. Joan and I spent the whole first day helping clean house. After that, we subscribed to the service, the property owners' association sends out a patrol. You're supposed to let them know when you'll be here." Zoey stopped abruptly and looked at Nora. "Oh, oh."

Nora held up her arm and looked at her watch in the light from the entry hall. "It's ten thirty. Probably too late to call now."

"I don't think anyone would be in the office. I don't want to call emergency when there isn't one. We'll call first thing in the morning. You cold?"

"Not at all, quite cozy. Kind of warm, in fact." Nora unwound the quilt a little.

"That's these quilts. They're fine for the winter when it gets down to zero, or the teens, but not much use the rest of the time." Zoey unwrapped herself, too. "I brought them out because they were in the cedar chest and I knew they wouldn't be dusty or smoky."

"Tell me some more, Zoe. More happy memories about this place." Nora drained the wine into Zoey's cup, and without even asking, opened another bottle.

"Whoever said the memories were happy? Don't jump to conclusions, Nore. I used to hate coming up here. Weekends weren't so bad, especially when we got older, but we used to come up for two weeks every summer for Dad's vacation. That was a nightmare."

"Really? Why Zoe?" Nora screwed up her face, on the edge of tears.

"You've met my mother and father. You know the answer to that question."

"You mean because they banter?"

"Banter!" Zoey slapped one knee with a hand. "That's hysterical! Banter, bicker, snipe, argue. I guess it doesn't matter," she sighed. "The thing is, that is their normal form of communication. They never stop, never. What saves them at home is that they aren't together very much, even on the weekends. She has bridge and her garden club and attorneys' wives association. They put on charity dinners and golf tournaments. He has poker, golf, spends lots of the time at the country club watching football, stuff like that. So this place is a monument, really, to their all-encompassing, enduring, enmity towards each other."

Zoey, once started down this stony, stony road, could not seem to stop. "You saw that atrocious light fixture hanging from the rafters. It's sort of part satellite, part star? Well, we call that 'father's revenge.' My mom bought a chandelier to hang there to replace whatever was there. She said it was because she wanted more light, but we all knew that she got it to annoy him. It was formal and huge and cut crystal and belonged at the Doge's Palace. It did not belong here. Was completely out of place. But that was the point. Mom hated roughing it. She hated the way this place was furnished, and especially hated everything that he loved. She ordered monogrammed towels with lace hems, he took them out in the boat fishing. She couldn't bear to eat off the table and insisted on place mats. He thought that was ridiculous but, you know, he probably would have gone for wooden slats, or reed, or even those straw ones. But, would she go there? Settle for that? Just wait until tomorrow. Wait till you see our place mat collection: mother of pearl, white organdy with hemstitching, another poufy round organdy set, assorted lace ones." Zoey had to laugh.

"What about your dad? Didn't he get upset?"

"Oh, sure. But he wouldn't react, not by making a fuss. Oh, he used to get his glass caught in some of the more elaborate ones and accidentally spill, especially red wine. But he bided his time, got her good with the bar-b-que smoker set he gave her for Christmas. It came complete with a dozen metal plates. Those sectioned ones, each one a different color with tumblers and bowls to match. She was furious. Despised them. Never used them. But every time he bar-b-queued, which was almost every night in the summer, out they came," Zoey laughed. "To add insult to injury he never failed to call out from the kitchen, 'name your color, ladies.' Joanie always picked red and pouted if she couldn't have it. I usually took silver or gold, the champion colors. Mom always said 'surprise me' as snidely as possible. Even as little kids, Joan and I knew what was going on, and even though we sometimes laughed at them, at the lengths they would go to get each other, it wasn't fun. It wasn't happy."

"But I've been to your home so many times and it's lovely. It's very nicely done and your parents were perfectly normal with each other."

"Aha! And that's the crazy making part. As long as they are playing their roles for others, that's how they behave: pillar of the community, successful partner of his law firm. And over-achieving charitable patroness of the arts and culture, as well as dutiful hostess, helpmate, wife and mother – living quietly in their upscale, refined home. See my father would never question my mother when it came to furnishing or decorating their home. He defers to her in all matters. This isn't about that. The issue here is roughing it. He has an image of what that means, and what this place is about. She won't abide by it. It's only one of the battlefields of their war."

"God, Zoe, I had no idea. I mean, you tend to think everybody was raised like you were, then you hear this kind of stuff." Nora was at a loss.

"Yes, well, on a scale of one to ten I didn't have it so bad. At least not compared to what some of my patients have told me. I did feel sorry for Joanie, though. She was enough younger, it was harder for her. She always had an asthma attack, always stepped on broken glass, always got bitten by mosquitoes, stung by bees. If there was poison ivy within a mile, she got it. When Dad showed us how to chop kindling with an ax, she hit herself in the knee and we had to take her to get stitches. When she caught a fish she cried. She couldn't stand to watch them being cleaned, wouldn't eat them for anything and cried herself to sleep almost every night."

"God! How sad!"

"Yeah. I vacillated between feeling like that, sad and sorry for her and feeling like she was acting like a baby." Zoey sighed. "I was right on both counts, of course. They were turning her into a baby, both of them. By using her in their battle plans, they forced her into that role. Meanwhile, I was the big girl. I did as was expected and more so. I learned to fish, to tie flies, to cast. I got up at the crack of dawn and wore waders and tinkered with the outboard engine on the boat. I sucked it up and removed hooks, cut fishes heads off and gutted them. Dad and I laughed at Mom and Joan. I enjoyed it in a way, and Dad and I got closer than we would have if it weren't for this place I guess, but then..." Zoey's voice trailed off and she was quiet for a long time lost in thought. Finally, as though coming back from another place, she went on. "Later, when I came out, he acted so betrayed. Couldn't even look at me, let alone try to understand. I argued, then I reasoned, then I cried, begged. I did everything I could think of." Zoey's voice had become a whisper. "It took me years. Years and years to understand that he felt responsible and guilty. He thought that it was his fault. That somehow, teaching me to chop wood and fly cast and follow a trail, that somehow, I turned out to be gay because of that."

"Oh, my God, Zoe. But surely your mom could..."

"Oh, he would never admit that. I'm not sure he even knew it on a conscious level. I don't think Mom ever guessed either although if she did, I wouldn't put it past her to reinforce his feelings."

"Come on Zoey. She surely wouldn't have bought into that. She's far too smart and compassionate. I thought she was always supportive of you."

"She has been, from the get go. She loves us. Joan and me, and wants to be there for us. Still she might have encouraged Dad's feelings of responsibility. You know what they say, Nore, people do terrible things to each other in a war."

Nora was unnerved. She didn't want to pry, but, "Why do you think they stayed together Zoe for all this time?"

"Because in their own weird way they love each other. They just relate on such a confrontational level. He says white, she says black. He says stop, she says go. They can't help it; probably that's what attracted them to each other. They seem to thrive on it."

Nora stood up. "I'll be right back. Time for another pill, so I'll go to the john and test for smoke."

"Okay," Zoey yawned, "keep the hall door shut. I'm trying to keep as much smoke as possible from the bathroom and bedrooms. It should be easing up by now. I opened every window."

"Oh, dear. I hope critters don't come in," Nora laughed nervously.

"Don't worry about that. The screens were already up; a pleasant surprise. That was one of the things I was going to do this weekend."

Nora returned, sneezing, a few minutes later. "It's still pretty bad in there."

Zoey stuck a finger in her mouth and held it up in the air. "What little breeze there is, is coming straight at us. We need to keep this door wide open." She got up and opened the front door all the way and then closed the screen door again. I have just got to turn in. The question is where. Did you check the bedrooms?"

"Not really, but the john is just the same as the living room. I couldn't tell any difference."

"I'll go check it out."

While she was gone, Nora fiddled with her chair. She discovered that it not only folded up, but also unfolded into several positions. She could gradually lower the back and thrust the seat forward until she was almost lying flat on her back. By the time Zoey returned, she had decided on a position about half way between, about a forty-five degree angle.

"Oh, good! You already discovered the adjustable chairs." This time Zoey had brought pillows with her. "It's still pretty bad in there. We have our choice, I guess; either sleep in the car, sleep right here or..."

"Or what?" Nora anxiously awaited her third choice.

"Or I could go under the house and find the tent that hasn't been used for a least ten years, and is probably mildewed, full of spiders, and smelling like a wet dog." Zoey flashed Nora that grin and they both began to settle in for the night.

Nora stuffed a pillow behind her back and one under her head and covered up with the quilt. "Actually, I'm really comfortable."

Zoey lay on her side with the back of the chair cranked as far back as it would go. She stuck one pillow under her head and another between her legs. "Night, Nore. Thanks for chauffeuring me all over today. Thanks especially for bringing me all the way up here. I'm sorry about the smoke and everything. I owe you big time."

"I've enjoyed it, Zoe. Enjoyed it all. Today...coming up here. Even this, right now. It was fun, just being with you." As she said it, and she realized how much she meant it, Nora cried, she couldn't help it.

Zoey realized how much she meant it too and she also cried; she couldn't help it either.

13

They slept fitfully. Napped really. Nora imagined she heard buzzing and furtive critter skittering.

Zoey imagined they slept right through a snowstorm with brusque winds, and they awoke to find the cabin full of snow three feet deep. "But the screens, the window screens should have kept the snow out!" she had wailed plaintively.

Zoey woke up for real about six o'clock when a dusty, beige pickup truck rumbled loudly up the road. She pulled up slightly on an elbow as she watched it turn off the road onto their drive and pull up to a stop dead in front of the cabin. A man in a cowboy hat, plaid wool jacket and jeans opened the door and climbed down.

"Joan? Willy? That you guys?"

Zoey sat straight up and Nora began to awaken as he moved closer to the cabin. "Joan?" he repeated.

"No, I'm her sister, Zoey."

"Oh! I thought there must have been some trouble. Them back here, already. They only just left yesterday afternoon."

By now, he was at the bottom of the steps and Zoey had thrown off her quilt and stood at the top. "Nice to meet you, Zoey. You must be the doctor I've heard so much about, I'm Dillen Parks, with the homeowner's association. Most folks around her just call me Dill."

"Hi, Dill," Zoey stuck out her hand, repressing the urge to say 'Howdy.' This is my friend Nora. We got here last night, late, and I made a fire without opening the damper on the flue. You know the rest." Zoey made a face. "Had to sleep out here all night."

85

Dill pushed his hat back on his head and laughed. "Happens to us all, one time or 'nother. So you dint see your sister or your cousin Willy? I think they left around three or four. They was gonna try to beat the traffic and leave early, but you know how that goes. You gotta do one more thing, then another."

Zoey was just about to interrupt him and ask discreetly about cousin Willy when Nora did it for her.

"Willy? I never heard of him! Have I ever met him?"

Dill began laughing and winking at Zoey, before she could respond. "Him! I recken she's never met cousin Willy, all right! That's a good one. Cousin Willy, a him!"

Nora and Zoey exchanged a look, eyebrows in the sky.

"So my sister just left yesterday?"

"Yep, same as usual. Up Tuesday morning, home Thursday afternoon. Only this time they came earlier. Came up late Monday night and stayed a little later, that's cause they had so much to do. They're having a gang up here next weekend. I guess you know. Wanted to have everything ship shape."

Zoey's eyes were huge. "That's the reason I came up, to help out. I didn't realize Joan would come up ahead of time."

Dill gave her a funny look. "You ain't been up here much lately, huh!"

Zoey shook her head. "Not the last year or so."

"That's what I thought. Well your sister and your cousin…they been coming up most every week since March. Since they plowed the road in, and last year." Dill scratched his head. "Last year I think they only missed a couple of weeks clear till Thanksgiving."

"And Willy always comes with my sister?"

"Always. Always has since I been up here. Be four years this July, and they always call in and let us know."

"I'm sorry Dill. It was a real last minute decision. I didn't even think about coming until seven last night. Had I planned earlier, I would have called."

"And I would have told you your sister was here and we could have avoided your smoke problem. How bad is it?"

"Let's find that out right now," Zoey turned around and opened the screen as she spoke.

"Doesn't seem too bad." Dill lifted his nose and sniffed like a rabbit. "Still a smoky residue in the air." He ran a finger over the tabletop. "No point in washing all this down till you clear the air. Too bad; your sister 'bout killed herself vacuuming all the furniture, polishing the wood, waxing the floors. I could go over to Jake the plumber's, and borrow a couple of his big fans, blow it out good in a couple hours."

"Oh, would you, Dill?" Zoey pulled her wallet out of her purse.

"Oh, he won't charge you, Dr. Hennessey. Not for a little wear and tear on his fans. You'll pay, though. You'll pay through the nose when you get your electric bill."

"It doesn't look like I have a choice, and please call me Zoey. I'd offer you breakfast Dill, but I don't know what, if anything, we have. I was going to take Nora into Lillian's this morning to eat, and then shop next door for what we needed. It's sort of a family tradition with us."

"Yep. Joan and Willy most always do that, too. Tell ya what. I'll go get them fans while you two freshen up and make your shopping list. Then I'll set a while here, have my coffee and read the paper and guard your house while you all go into Lillian's and do your shopping."

In his absence, Zoey made a surprisingly long list, mostly cleaning supplies. "Joan must have brought everything with her and then taken it home again. Shit, we're gonna need a bucket of 409!"

"Get some rubber gloves too, Zoe. No point in ruining our nails."

"Do you realize how ludicrous this is? I never clean anything, except myself, and here I am," Zoey looked around, exasperated. "Polly would take one look at this place, throw her hands in the air and say, 'thanks…but no thanks.'"

Nora came of out the john in the nude. "There's no water Zoe. None. Not even a little dribble."

After a brief affirmation of this dismal truth and a subsequent confrontation with the water supply line, Zoey realized what had happened. "Remember last night when no water came out in the kitchen and you drank your pill down with wine? That's because the water was already on. Sure! They wouldn't turn it off. Not in May, for Christ's sake! It was on. I turned it off." She went into the kitchen to test her theory and was rewarded by a couple of coughs from the sink faucet, then a low rumble and sudden gush of water, which slowed itself down to a moderate stream. "Go ahead. You can take a shower if you want. There might not be any hot, or if there is some, it might run out."

Even Zoey's spotlight grin was not enough to convince Nora to take that chance.

By seven thirty they were driving to Lillian's, having left the cabin with every window open and two huge fans going in the living room. Dill had brought three fans but every time he turned on the third one, he blew a fuse. He was still looking for somewhere to plug it in when they left, and his last words to them were yelled from the front porch. "Bring back some fuses!"

"That's kind of funny about Joan, huh, and Cousin Willy, coming up here for so long. Do you think there's something going on there? Think maybe Willy's more than just a cousin?"

"I don't think so, Nore, I know so. I mean, I don't know if Willy is more than a cousin or less than a cousin, all I do know is what Willy is not, and that's a cousin."

"No shit?" Nora gave Zoey a look.

"I do not know Willy," Zoey grinned ear to ear. "I do not know what Willy is to my sister, only what she is not. In fact, I had no clue Willy was a she until Dill said she was. I obviously know as little about my sister's love life as I do about her coming up here. I didn't realize how out of touch I was."

They drove the rest of the way in thoughtful silence and Nora watched as a small smile played around Zoey's mouth.

As the front door accidentally slammed behind them, Zoey spied Lillian through the window into the kitchen. "Zoey? Zoey Hennessey! It does these old eyes good just to look at you, honey! Lord! It's been years and years, but I'd know you anywhere. Course your hair's a lot darker; used to be white, you know," she said in an aside to Nora, as if they were old friends.

"Good to see you, Lillian," Zoey hugged her. "I am surprised you recognized me, though."

"I swear, I'd know you anywhere. Even if Dillen hadn't a told me you was comin in."

"That's exactly what I thought!" Zoey laughed and slid into a booth. "This is my friend Nora. We came up to do some serious fishing."

"Well, I hear tell Perish Creek and Goo Pond are bein' stocked yesterday and today." Lillian came out from behind the counter with two mugs of coffee. "You ladies look like you could use some of this. Rough night, huh?"

Zoey nodded and reached for her mug. "Dillen told you, I suppose," she smirked at Lillian. "I was just kidding about the fishing, Lillian. We really did come up here to clean the cabin. Looks like that's just what we'll be doing."

"No need to look at the menu. I know what you'll be havin, the lumberjack special."

"Oh, I don't know, Lillian. I don't think…"

"Don't be silly. That's what you always have. Ever since you sat in a booster chair."

"Well, I know. But there's no way I..."

Zoey threw her hands helplessly into the air as Lillian marched into the kitchen. "Two lumberjack specials comin up," she announced to the otherwise empty coffee shop.

"You want to guess why I've always had the same thing here?"

Nora was amused. A silly smile plastered across her face. It widened when Lillian served them and grew larger watching Zoey glare at the food. First came eggs, ham, toast and hash brown potatoes. Then came bacon and a short stack of hotcakes. Nora began to laugh merrily at the look on Zoey's face.

"Lillian," she finally called, "Zoey and I need doggie bags." Lillian came out from the kitchen, frowning. "Well, we left Dillen guarding the house. All the windows open and all, and he's too busy. Can't wait around for us forever. So, how about we finish off our eggs and potatoes and you pack up all the rest for us while we run next door for some supplies. Then, we can finish breakfast at home and get Dillen on his way."

This seemed to pacify Lillian, as well as being a stroke of genius as far as Zoey was concerned. A fact that she expounded on during the drive back to the cabin.

"That was really clever, Nora. I never would have thought of it. Now we can pitch the rest of the food without hurting Lillian's feelings."

"The hell we will! That's lunch, Zoe. We won't have to stop work, go anywhere or fix anything."

They arrived back at the wind tunnel to find Dillen sitting out on the porch with his coffee and paper, as advertised. He looked at his watch. "Only eight thirty, I figure we got at least another hour, hour and a half. Put one of the fans upstairs. It was bad up there. You're gonna have to wash all of them bedspreads, all six of 'em. Maybe the downstairs ones, too, though they don't seem so bad. Lucky you didn't uncover any of the upholstered furniture in the living room. It'll probably be fine. I already pulled the rugs out and hung them on the line. Beat 'em real good. They can just air out all day. Took down your screens for ya, too. They need to be scrubbed up and re-hung. Y'all scrub 'em and I'll hang them back up when I come back to get the fans."

"Sounds like a plan. I'll go start on the bedspreads."

Dillen shook his head. "Not with the fans goin'. Why don't I take the whole mess of 'em in to the Laundromat. I'll bring 'em back when I come for the fans."

"That would be a big help, Dill. Then we'll scrub the screens."

Dillen nodded. "They's all leaning against the cabin right by the window they fit on. Be careful not to mix 'em up or you'll be in a real pickle."

14

By ten Zoey and Nora had finished the screens. There was nothing else they could think of to do until Dill came to turn off the fans, so they set their chairs up on the front walk where they were in the sun, and a little farther away from the noisy fans. Zoey brought soft drinks from the kitchen and Nora had rescued their purses from the dining table.

"It's a lot better in there. I didn't even cough getting our bags," she reported to Zoey, who had gone in and out the back door.

"Unbelievable! I can't believe all we've done already, and it's only ten in the morning."

"I look like the wrath of God!" Nora began brushing her hair. "Did you sleep at all last night?"

"I guess I must have, but it sure doesn't feel like it. How about you?"

Nora shook her head. "I can't wait for Dill to come get those fans so we can finish up and crash."

"We might have an hour or two wait. Maybe we should try to sleep now."

"I could try. I'm so tired. I wish I hadn't had all that coffee, though. Before I do one other thing, I have to check my messages and my service."

"Oh, God! The seminar! Aw shit! It's ten?"

Nora calmly handed Zoey the phone. "Be my guest. You call first."

Zoey dug out her daily calendar and punched in a number. Introducing herself, she began to explain her absence at the seminar. "That's perfectly understandable, Dr. Hennessey. Roxanne Morgan filled us in earlier regarding your emergency."

Then Zoey called her service and listened, fast forwarding as she went through five messages. Then she called her machine at home. The first message was from her sister. Zoey raised her eyebrows and hit speakerphone so Nora could hear. "Hi, Zoe. It's Joan. It's almost nine o'clock Thursday night and I'm surprised you aren't there. I just wanted to chat, really, nothing important. Don't call me back tonight, I'm on my way over to Mom and Dad's. The doctor's think he may have suffered another stroke. They're not sure, but if he has, it's a very, very minor one, no big deal. I'm only going over myself to scope out the lay of the land."

"St. Joan dealeth out the guilt." Zoey held the phone up. "Mind if I call her?"

"God! Of course not! Please!"

"Joan Hennessey."

"Joan. It's Zoey! I just now got your message. What's up with Dad? Is he okay?"

"He's fine Zoe. As fine as he can be, in his condition. I told you, if he had a stroke, and they still don't know if he did, it was a very small one."

"But if they don't know for sure, what makes them think he might have had one?"

"Because of his increased, um, disability, inability really, to express himself clearly. He can't seem to communicate, say what he wants to say. And he gets so angry."

"You mean, he can't talk?"

"Oh, he can talk, all right. But what he says is inappropriate sometimes. He called Mrs. Hapwell, from next door, a fat old cow. And he called the gardeners dirty Japs. They aren't even Japanese, luckily. They're Puerto Ricans, so at least they weren't mad just bewildered."

"But physically he seems okay?"

"Fine, Zoe. That is the weird thing. His blood pressure is down, his cholesterol is down, the ulcer is gone completely. Dr. Maddux said he has the constitution of a kid."

"That's because he is a kid, Joanie. That's what he has become inside," Zoey said softly.

"I know, I know," Joan whispered. "He's still very fragile, bone-wise," she added, "and of course, a hemorrhage could come at any time."

"Then we have to be grateful for what we do have. Mom's staying busy?"

"Yes! I spent the night there last night. Mom was out of there at eight this morning, meetings in the city. Some fashion show, luncheon and then a planning committee meeting for the big Sons of Ireland dinner next weekend. We tried to call you this morning before she left, to let you know Dad's okay but you still weren't home."

"No! You won't believe where I was, still am, in fact." Zoey went on to fill her in.

"Oh, Zoey, I'm so sorry. I should have told you I was up there. That everything was in order. I never dreamed you'd think of going. You haven't gone up for ages."

"Hey, no problem! I came up to clean, and that's what I'm doing."

"Well don't knock yourself out. I may not even be coming up. When you called, I was just sitting here thinking I'd better cancel the whole thing."

"But why? You've planned this for months."

"Listen, you don't have to tell me, but it isn't the end of the world. We can do it another time. It's because of the Sons of Ireland dinner."

"What?" Zoey hit the fan. "Why the hell do you have to go to that?"

"Well, I wasn't going to but now, well now Mom has a problem. She has taken a table for eight. She had to, Zoey. He's one of the honorees. And she can't have any empty chairs at the table. And, she has to be super careful who she invites to sit there. Besides the two of them, there are Dad's two caretakers, Chuck and Jay. They usually trade off, except on occasion when they might both be needed, like Saturday night. Then, Mom was going to fill in with some young clerks in the firm. She figured she could at least count on their loyalty. But he's become so bad at times, bawdy but funny on the crudest level, belching and farting, too."

"Oh, dear God!"

"Right! It would be all over the legal community, let alone the city. So I guess I'll go, with a date, and my friend Willy said she would bring a date and go, too. It's all we can think of to do."

"I don't want you to do that Joan, especially after all the work you've put in and now I have, too, here at the cabin. You can't cancel. Don't worry! I'll talk to Mom. I'll go myself," Zoey declared impulsively.

"Oh, Zoe. God I don't know. Just seeing you might set him off."

"Well that's just too God damn bad if it does, the old bastard. This is no longer your problem Joan, I mean it."

"Are you sure Zoey?"

"Real sure!"

"Call Mrs. Babbitt. Maybe she or one of her kids can come over and help you clean. They're always looking for extra money. I hate to think of you scouring away all on your own."

"That's a good idea. I might just do that. But I'm not alone. Nora's with me." Zoey put her hand over the phone. "Sorry," she mouthed to Nora who smiled and shrugged.

There was stunned silence for several seconds. "Nora? Nora Fairchild?"

"The very one." Zoey leered at Nora.

"Oh, Zoe. I had no idea. I'm so happy for you. Does Mom know?"

"No, Joan. It's not...not like that. Just don't mention it, okay?'

"I understand Zoey. Don't worry. Your secret is safe with me. Been there, done that."

Was that a hint? A little bait? Should she ask Joan whatever did she mean? The therapist within her would not let Zoey do that. "I'll talk to you soon, Joan. And don't worry about next week. When do you plan to come up?"

"Wednesday, right after lunch. Everyone else is coming up Thursday. That'll give Willy and me plenty of time to get organized."

"There it was, the bait again. This time perfectly placed, impossible to miss." Zoey knew it was only a matter of time, probably the next phone call, before Joanie gave up on the bait and went for the straight hook.

Zoey said, "Goodbye," and sat, staring at the phone "Now I've gone and done it."

"I thought it was a real stand up call, Zoe. So kind and generous. And, at the same time, sort of heroic; not letting your sister be punished for something totally out of her control."

"Well, thanks for that, for seeing it that way. That's where I hope I'm coming from. I'm also so pissed at Mom for even involving Joan. You notice she didn't ask me."

"Well, but Joan's right there and you aren't."

"Right! I'm almost two whole hours away," Zoey went on bitterly. "No, what Joan said is true. Just seeing me might set Dad off. He's so angry Nore." Zoey picked up a pebble and threw it as hard as she could. "Even in his lunacy, he's so pissed at me, betrayed, hurt, bitter and guilty."

"He's wacko! You can't let how he feels bother you."

"I know. But I'm drawing the line at my little sister." Zoey punched in her home number again. "My machine said I had four messages but I panicked after Joanie's. I better see who the others are. Funny, now the line is busy."

"Probably someone else leaving you a message."

Dill surprised them, earlier than expected. "You are a real life saver, Dill." Zoey couldn't remember ever having been so glad to see anyone!

They went immediately to work. Starting in the loft, they swabbed down all the hard surfaces, put the clean spreads on all the beds and washed the windows. Then, they did the same downstairs. Zoey had considered calling Mrs. Babbitt but decided against it. Nora agreed.

"I don't know what it is exactly, but it feels good doing this—therapeutic."

"That's because you can actually see what you are accomplishing. It's visually rewarding." Zoey gave the table she was polishing one more swipe and grinned with satisfaction.

Dill finished hanging the screens and got insulted when Zoey tried to give him money for doing it. "You gave me more'n enough for the laundry, Zoey."

"Two dollars more. Come on Dill!"

"Come on yourself. I don't take money for helping friends." With that and a wave, he backed his car down to the road and was off.

Nora and Zoey heated up the pancakes, ham and sausage, and had it for lunch. Then, while Zoey was cleaning up, Nora eyed her cell phone. "I almost hate to do this. For a while I forgot all about Gabriella! But I guess I better see if I have any messages. Shit! I do."

Zoey dried her hands and came to the kitchen table. Sitting across from Nora she laid her hands palms down, on the tabletop. "Go ahead, bound to be one from best friend Sybil. Sock it to me."

Nora put it on speaker and turned up the volume. They made faces at each other as they heard Sybil's voice. "Hi Nora! Sorry to bother you but I really feel you should know what happened here, at the house tonight. I met Clyde for dinner after work, the Thursday night combo at Styro's. Afterwards we each had our own cars and I followed Clyde home. When he slowed to turn into the driveway his headlights hit a parked car and I saw a woman behind the wheel. I recognized her right off as Gabriella and, while I was waiting for the garage door to open and Clyde to pull in, I pulled up next to her and rolled down the window to say hello. She was horrified, like I had caught her doing something embarrassing, so I tried to make her feel comfortable. 'If you're looking for Nora, she isn't here,' I told her. She said she had been calling and calling you and you weren't taking her calls. She thought you were using your caller ID. I said, no, that you had your phone turned off for the night and to leave you a message and I was sure you would return her call. Then I had to tell her why it was turned off. You told me to tell her, Nora, about Zoey's house call. That's when she sort of lost it. She started crying and said, 'Did you hear that?' really loud to somebody else in the car. Until then I didn't know anybody else was in the car. I barely caught sight of her, but I know it was that Chris, Zoey's friend the writer. Anyway, then I just said I was sure you'd be back by tomorrow sometime, and, nice to see you again. Then she took off like a bat outta hell, laying rubber. Clyde wanted to know who my NASCAR friends were. That's about all, except, Clyde and I didn't go right to sleep, if you know what I mean. About midnight, about ten minutes ago, I got up to get a drink of water. The lights were all out and the sliding door from the living room to the deck was open and I went outside. They were back, Nore. No doubt about it. The moon was super bright and I could see them in the car, both of them. It kind of gave me the creeps."

"It kinda gives me the creeps, too," Nora whispered.

Zoey took a deep breath and looked at Nora. "Obsession...possession...fixation...stalking...It totally gives me the creeps."

Nora frowned and wrinkled her nose. "What is this one?" she wondered, not recognizing the number on the screen.

"Nore...Norie," the voice was barely audible and they had to strain to hear it. Then they clearly heard sobbing. "Oh...oh...God...Nora...where are you. I want my sister. I think I'm in labor and they won't give me anything because of the baby. Rick is in Japan and I haven't been able to reach him, and I'm all alone here. Call me when you get this, no matter what time it is," more sobbing. "I...I need to talk to you Norie." Nora stared at the phone, re-wound the message and played it and then rewound the message and played it again.

Then she called the number on the display. "It's Bonnie's cell. I don't think I've ever called her on it. 'The mobile customer you are trying to reach is currently unavailable. Please try again later.' Nora called her Mom and Dad, no answer. She hung up without leaving a message and tried Bonnie and Rick's, thinking that's where they were, with the kids. There was no answer there but she did leave a message. Then she called her parents' and left another message, and fast-forwarded over the other two messages on her cell phone. One of them was from Gabriella. 'Call me when you can,' and suddenly not so very important.

"We could start calling hospitals," Zoey was trying to think. "How many do you suppose there are?"

"Who knows? Maybe a hundred in the whole area. I mean I haven't a clue. Don't know her doctor's name." Nora ran her fingers through her hair. "All I can do is wait until someone calls me." Nora began pacing around. "I'll go crazy, just waiting."

"You should go, Nore, just go. Where's the nearest airport? I'll take you there and drive your car home."

"It'd be faster to just damn drive all the way than drive to the airport and then wait around till the next flight. You're right though, I'll go crazy if I don't do something. Come on. Let's load up and lock up. I'll take you home and go on from there."

15

They were in the car and almost to where the road met the larger road, at the non-existent big yellow house. Nora was prepared to turn right when Zoey touched her arm.

"I can't let you, Nore. I can't let you take me home. All that way. It's at least an hour and a half. Hell, it's only another hour from here to your folks."

"Don't be silly, Zoe. You don't need to do that."

"Yes, Nora. Yes I do. I don't want to have to worry about you driving all that way alone. Two and a half hours from here, verses four hours if you take me home and go from there. You're already exhausted and we don't know what you're walking into. I want to come."

Nora stopped the car. "No shit?"

Zoey drove for the first leg of the journey as she knew, more or less, how to get from White Lake to civilization going the opposite direction from the way they had come.

"What we have here essentially is an isosceles triangle," Nora studied a map. "Here's White Lake. Here's where we came from and here's where we're going. Here's the way we'll go home. Quite a little drive. You're sure you want to do this?"

"I'm sure. I don't have anything else I need to do, until the Sons of Ireland dinner," her smile was wicked and sly.

"Oh, I get it. Okay. It's a deal. I'll go with you if you want me to."

"Never mind, I'm only teasing. It just struck me funny. I haven't seen you for two days in a row for the last four years, until the night before last. Now we've been sort of thrown together ever since then. It's so odd."

"Fate, Zoe, Karma. I meant what I said last night," Nora continued shyly. "I've enjoyed it, really. Being with you again has been fun."

"Well, that's because I planned our fun, built it in so well. The ease of finding the cabin; going back and forth on the highway so many times; filling the place with smoke; turning the water off instead of on; sleeping in folding chairs on the porch," Zoey laughed out loud.

"And don't forget the prehistoric, petrified animal feces."

"Oh, that is yours, my dear. Your own special memory to treasure."

"Because you didn't touch it!"

Once they negotiated their way down the mountains, they stopped to get gas, stretch their legs and get two large iced teas, which Zoey held while Nora got behind the wheel.

"I almost forgot. I ought to check my messages. Shit," Nora frowned at Zoey. "The phone's dead. Look in the glove box, would you? I'm pretty sure my charger is in there."

"This do-hickey?" Zoey plugged it into the cigarette lighter.

Once on the interstate, they were able to make pretty good time. "Check the phone again, would you. Somebody should have called me back by now. They would know I'd be worried."

"Nope! Nothing! They're probably all at the hospital. Haven't received your message."

"But they should have tried to call me."

"Maybe they're waiting Nora. They don't know anything yet and so they're waiting until something happens or they find out some thing, to call you."

"Maybe, or something has happened. Something bad and they keep calling, hoping I'll answer, because it's something they don't want to have to tell me in a message."

"Nore, don't, okay? Don't go there. Besides, if it was something like that they would still leave a message, just like Gabriella did, 'Call me.'"

"I know. I'm sorry. I'm just worried...and..."

"Exhausted," Zoey finished for her. "We both are. All the drama of the last two days, on top of no sleep last night. It reminds me of Hell Week when I was in college."

"That's it, exactly!" Nora slapped the top of the steering wheel. "Feeling all jittery and jumpy inside. Not being able to think a complete thought."

"And at the absolute edge of emotional control, ready to collapse at any second." Zoey handed Nora her iced tea, "Here. The caffeine will do you good, at least temporarily."

They began to hit traffic at two-thirty. By three they were stuck in bumper to bumper, stop and go, a nightmare for the sleep deprived. They should have arrived at the Fairchild residence at three thirty. Instead, it was almost four thirty when they got there.

"Mom's home," Nora announced. "At least the front door's open and her car is here." Nora continued up the driveway and parked in the double carport next to the garage, where she had been parking her car since her seventeenth birthday.

"Mom...Mom," she called, letting the back porch screen door slam.

"Nora?" her mother's astounded voice preceded her from the bathroom. In her housecoat, she appeared at the hall door, washcloth in one hand, towel in the other. "Nora! I can't believe it! When did you...How did you..."

"Bonnie called me," Nora managed to get out, before her mother's arms encircled her. They continued to hug, rubbing each other's backs. Nora went on, "I tried calling everywhere, I left messages. She sounded so scared Mom. I couldn't think what else to do, so we decided to just come."

"Nora's mom pushed back from her and looked at her. "We?" and then she turned around. It was an instantaneous reaction. Tears squirted out of her eyes, and she began to tremble. Then, she began to sob as she reached for her. "Zoey...oh my God!"

Surprised, and a little overcome herself, Zoey embraced her.

"Oh, my God. Forgive me. I'm sorry..." Nell whispered in Zoey's ear. "I never, ever, gave up, Zoey. I always knew that you and Nora would come to your senses someday. Thank God. Oh honey, you can't imagine how I've missed you, longed for you."

"I missed you too, Mrs. Fairchild," Zoey admitted truthfully, her eyes wide as she gave Nora a look over her Mom's shoulder.

"Please, honey. It's Nell. You girls must be hungry," she went on. Still clutching Zoey's hand, she led them into the kitchen. "I hope I didn't embarrass you Zoey. I'm just so surprised and so thrilled." Releasing her grip, she patted the back of Zoey's hand. "It's been an emotional couple of days for us, and so draining. You girls caught me about to rinse my face with cold water, trying to wake up from a nap."

Nora took the washcloth from her mom, dampened it and returned it to her as the three of them sat at the kitchen table.

"We were at the hospital all night. Bonnie was asleep. I wanted to be there for her if she woke up. Dad slept, too, sitting upright in a chair, a pillow shoved between his head and the wall. I don't see how he does it."

Nora and Zoey smiled at each other. "Sounds familiar. That's just what we did, Mom. It's a long story. We'll have to fill you in later. Tell me about Bonnie."

"Well, you know she went into labor. She's at Saint Mary of the Plains, where she had the other two, and Doctor O'Connor has sent for the Monsignor who advises on fetus viability for the Diocese. He arrives about eight tonight, and he'll advise on…well, the viability of the fetus." Nell dropped the washcloth onto the table.

"What? What kind of bullshit is this!" Nora exploded. "What do you mean he's arriving, if he's the Diocese expert."

"Just what I said, honey. I guess we share his expertise with several other Diocese. I think they said he's from Boston."

"Well, what does he have to do with everything."

Nell pursed her lips. "We, um, haven't been able to get a hold of Rick, yet. I guess Bonnie told you, he's in Japan. They're tracking him down. I know if he were here, none of this would be happening. But, well, St. Mary's is not only a Catholic hospital, but also a teaching Catholic hospital. The head of the whole hospital, a neurosurgeon, is a Nun."

"So? I'm not following this Mom. So what?"

"I think what your mom means is that the doctor is hesitant to give Bonnie medication because it might harm the fetus. And if the fetus is viable it must be allowed to be born prematurely. No matter what the consequences to the mother or the baby."

Nell nodded her head and held the damp cloth to her face. "They won't even give her pain medication," she said through the washcloth.

"Well, Mom! That is just ludicrous! We don't have to put up with that bull!"

"It's your sister's wish. She doesn't want to rock the boat. You know, Rick's parents. They're so devout. They've always considered Bonnie the weak link, the convert."

"What about Bonnie? What if something were to happen to her? What about the kids?" Nora stopped. "Where are the kids?"

"Dad is picking them up at Rick's sister's at five-thirty. Cassie said she'd feed them. Then he'll bring them here. I'll give them a bath and get them ready for bed before I go back to the hospital. All Papa has to do is put them in bed."

"Then he'll stay here with the kids? Put them to bed?"

"Oh, he'll be fine. He's done it before, for naps, but what's the difference?"

"The difference is now I'm here," Zoey declared. "I'll stay here with the kids. You guys all go. No! I mean it, Nore. Your sister needs you. You all need to be together at a time like this."

Nora and Zoey unloaded the car, bringing in only what they knew they would need, which included the ice chest full of wine.

"What's this," Nell laughed, "you don't think we have acceptable wine around here?" Then she saw the swordfish "What on earth?"

"It's fresh, Mom. I was going to barbecue last night but then we left sort of spur of the moment. I didn't want to freeze it."

"Well, do you want to cook it? Right now?" Nell held the fish in her hands.

"I don't. I'm not hungry. Zoe?" Zoey shook her head. "Well, maybe tomorrow."

"Yes, maybe tomorrow you'll feel like defrosting it and cooking it." Nell replied sticking it in the freezer. "It won't keep another day," she explained. "You girls will have to sleep in Bonnie's room. Your room, I'm afraid, is now the nursery honey."

"Fine," Nora said. Shit! is what she thought. Of course, it only made sense to put the kids in her room, with its twin beds. But she and Zoey? Sharing a double bed? Nora didn't think so! Thanks anyway. Peeking in her old room, Nora's fears went from bad to worse. There was only one bed set up, the other had been replaced by a crib.

Zoey seemed unfazed. The bed situation didn't even register with her and she busied herself with organizing their bathroom things.

They had just come back downstairs when Nora's dad arrived. He let the screen door bang, too, deposited Ritchy on the floor and turned around immediately to call out to the backyard. "Ellie? Ellie? Come on in with Papa, honey. This isn't a game. Papa doesn't have time to come looking for you, Ellie, Eleanor O'Riley! You come in here this minute!"

"Here I am, Dad!" Nora snuck up behind him and threw her arms around him.

Stunned as he was, Wade managed to hold tight to his daughter, Eleanor O'Riley the second, while her mother, the original of the species, went to find his granddaughter ,the third.

"Baby! Sweetheart! When did you get here. Nobody even told me you were coming."

"Because they didn't know, Dad. I didn't know. I just decided, just today."

For some reason, inhaling his scent, unwinding in the refuge of his arms, Nora was unable to hold on any longer. Losing it, she let herself go completely. "Daddy, Daddy, I'm so scared."

"Then I'm even more glad you're here where you belong. It'll be okay. You'll see, honey. Everything will be all right. We're all here. And we have each other. And that's what's important."

"Daddy," Nora sniffed, "you remember Zoey?" Nora and Wade turned as one, to find Zoey, fighting for control herself, and beginning to lose that fight.

"Sorry. Hi, Mr. Fairchild. I'm sorry. It's just that when Nora cries, it always makes me cry," Zoey shrugged and reached for the damp washcloth.

"I know just what you girls need. I never saw an agitated filly yet that couldn't be settled by some Kentucky Bourbon and branch water."

"Oh, no! No thanks! Really! I can't!" Both Zoey and Nora said at once. Zoey did end up having a glass of wine.

"What's this gobble-de-gook stuff? This what you want?"

Nora had a Coke. She needed the caffeine if she planned on remaining awake.

They sat again at the kitchen table and heard the back door shut and not slam. "Ellie? Ellie? Look who's here. Look who came to see us," Nell appeared in the kitchen doorway, Ritchy in her arms and Ellie holding onto her skirt.

"Auntie Nora! Auntie Nora!" Ellie screamed at the top of her lungs as she ran full speed at Nora, who caught her with both hands and lifted her high in the air before settling her in her lap. They kissed and kissed and hugged tightly.

Then Ellie looked up at her. "It's not my birthday and it's not Ritchy's birthday. We just had Daddy's birthday, and Mommy's is just before mine! Oh, oh," Ellie looked sad. "I hope it isn't Grammy or Papa's birthday," she continued in a stage whisper, "cause I didn't get them a present."

"That's okay, pumpkin. It isn't anyone's birthday. I just came to see you and Ritchy and...and everyone. I didn't bring a present either. Well, I sort of brought some thing. I brought you another aunt. Can you say hi to Aunt Zoey?"

Ellie turned around to look at Zoey. Huge blue eyes met their match and, as girls that age, three going on a precocious four, are apt to do, a quick assessment of the possibilities and an intuitive grasp of the probable rewards, clicked somewhere in Ellie's cognitive development. She had just successfully navigated the treacherous shoals of the second year of her life and, having completed her individuation process with flying colors, she now had a firm, enthusiastic sense of autonomy.

She held out her arms and very slowly and distinctly said, "My Aunt Zoey."

Stunned silence momentarily followed as Ellie went from Nora's to Zoey's arms. Tightening the lasso, and securing the knot, Ellie stood on Zoey's lap. One hand on each of Zoey's shoulders. She regarded her solemnly. "You're my Aunt Zoey." It was not a question, certainly not a demand of any kind, an affirmation, instantly responded to and re-affirmed.

"Yes, I am!" Zoey was choked up enough so that Nora and Nell both knew it.

"She never does that. I've never seen her do that. Papa, she never goes to strangers, does she. She's so shy, usually," Nell went on.

Zoey smiled strangely as Ellie touched her ears and her face and patted her hair.

"I'll go on and get started with him," Nell said. "I'll call you when it's time to bring Ellie up for her bath. "

Wade went into watch the baseball game and have another drink. Nora went to take a shower. And Zoey and Ellie stayed where they were, content in touching each other's hair, touching lips to cheeks, nose to nose and forehead to forehead. Getting to know each other. Getting to know a new kind of love.

Zoey took her upstairs just as Nora reappeared. "I'll take her into Mom. Now's your chance to hop in the shower," she said, taking off a terry cloth robe and tossing it to Zoey.

"That's sounds too good. Loan me a nightie, okay? I neglected to pack one," Zoey laughed.

Thirty minutes later Zoey and Ellie stood at the front door, waving, as the others left for the hospital.

"You're sure you'll be all right Zoey?" Nell's pinched face showed worries far greater than the one she voiced.

"Of course! We're fine! Aren't we Ellie! Don't worry! Bye!"

16

It was seven o'clock. Ritchy was down for the night and Ellie was due to join him at seven-thirty. Until then, Zoey was reading to her. She didn't want to turn on the TV because she didn't know how successful she might be in turning it off. As a matter of fact, she didn't know how successful she might be in disciplining this child at all, if it came to that. She sensed that any control she might have might depend entirely on the magnanimity of this mesmerizing, mini-monarch in her lap.

Indeed, Zoey deemed it to be in the best interest of all concerned to go with the flow and not make waves, as sorely as she was tempted. The temptation involved the books. Ellie had a whole basket full of books, but in that basket were certain favorites. Among those favorites were favorite pages. Those favorite pages were the approved reading material of the evening. Ellie did not find it necessary to wade through extraneous material to get to her good parts. Therefore, Zoey had read the same three or four pages from the same three or four books, over and over again. Every time Zoey attempted to read a couple of pages before or after or, God forbid, begin at the beginning, an autocratic little hand would snatch the book away and replace it immediately with one of the preferred pages. This went against all of Zoey's principles – begin at the beginning and proceed logically to the climax and the resolution. Besides, she would just like to know, damnit, why the other bunnies made fun of Droopy Ears. Did his ears droop like that because they made fun of him, an abuse reaction manifestation, or did they make fun of him because his ears drooped, a physical deformity provoking cruel discrimination. Things like that bothered Zoey, and she was thinking of taking a stand for continuity and order, when the phone rang.

Welcoming the diversion, she put her finger over her lips. "Be quite now so Aunt Zoey can answer the phone." Ellie put her own finger on her lips and nodded, her eyes round and huge.

Zoey answered, "Hello." She wished she had said 'Fairchild Residence.'

"Mrs. Fairchild?"

"No, I'm sorry she isn't here."

"Oh, well is Mr. Fairchild there?"

"I'm sorry none of them are here. I'm alone, staying with the children."

"Oh, I see. Are they at the hospital then?"

"Yes. Who's calling please?"

"I'm sorry. This is Gabriella Galanti and I need you to take a message for me. You see, Mrs. Fairchild called me, called my house, looking for her daughter Nora. She left a message, saying that there was a medical emergency involving her sister Bonnie and to please have Nora call home. Well, I've been trying and trying for the past two days to reach Nora." Zoey could hear Gabriella's voice spiraling out of control. "And I haven't been able to. I didn't want anyone to think I had disregarded Mrs. Fairchild's message. Will you tell them? Tell them I'll keep trying to reach Nora."

"You don't need to keep trying. She's here. Nora came today."

"Auntie Nora...Auntie Nora...Auntie Nora came today." Ellie began to chant.

"Shh.shh.Baby. Yes. Shh now," Zoey crooned.

"Oh, thank heavens! I couldn't imagine where she was. She just disappeared. I was beginning to worry. I'm so relieved. Will you send my love to her and the whole family?"

"Of course," Zoey said loudly, to be heard over Ellie's renewed chant.

"Auntie Nora came today. Auntie Nora came today."

"Sshh, sweetheart, shhh, shhh."

Then, inevitably, Ellie tired of this rivalry. She reached for the phone, trying to pull it away with her dimpled, little, possessive fingers. "You are my Aunt Zoey," she said clearly and proprietarily.

Zoey snatched the phone from Ellie. "I'll have Nora call you," she said crisply into the receiver. What she heard in return was a dial tone. Gabriella had hung up.

"Ellie and I probably cut her off while we wrestled over the phone," Zoey sincerely hoped. "She probably never even heard what Ellie said." She continued to rationalize, in spite of a sinking feeling in her stomach.

"Why is Ritchy making so much noise?"

"Because he's done!" Ellie told her. "He's quiet while he has his bottle, but then, when he's done, unless he's asleep, he stays up till I come. He gets lonesome for me so he starts rocking, till I come."

"Stays up? Rocking?"

"Yep! He stands up and rocks the crib. He can make it move far, doing that," Ellie elaborated with some pride.

"Well, let's go upstairs so we can be with him."

"Okay." Ellie sighed but didn't disagree. She did choose three books to take with them. "These are Ritchy's favorites," she explained.

At the top of the stairs, Ellie advised, "If you want to go potty, you better go now, because if you go in Ritchy's room and then leave again, he doesn't like it. He cries."

"Good tip. I'll just do that, thanks."

After sharing the facilities and brushing their teeth, they tiptoed into Ritchy's presence. "Love him and lay him down, but don't pick him up unless you wanna hold him," Ellie warned.

Zoey did just that. Then she pushed the crib back to its usual place along the wall, and she and Ellie lay down on the bed.

"Read this one for Ritchy. He'll go right to sleep."

"Okay. Then you read the next one," Zoey yawned and Ellie smirked and nodded, snuggling close.

Nora got in the elevator with her mom and dad. This hospital, lobby, entrance, and elevator felt so different. Nora had been in many hospitals, countless times. As an occupational therapist, a good deal of her practice involved, and revolved around, hospitals. So why did this seem so foreboding, so alien. "It must be because of mom and dad. I'm with them so I've assumed a part of their identity. I am no longer a working professional, within the complex, dealing with other working professionals. Instead, I am 'family of a patient,' to be treated cordially and compassionately, to be spoken to only if addressed. Then only in the broadest, most general terms; the weather, the traffic, sports perhaps. As far as specific questions concerning your loved one/patient, an all-purpose, 'Doctor will be better able to discuss that with you' was in order. Nora knew the routine. "She knew it all," as Zoey would say, "It was her job."

They got out of the elevator on the third floor and, waving and smiling at nurses and orderlies, went directly to Bonnie's room.

Nora was shocked at her sister's appearance. Even though she slept, her face reflected the suffering of acute pain. Her hair was plastered to her head, and her forehead was beaded with sweat.

A nurse stuck her head in the door and tapped her lips with her index finger. Nora followed her out into the hall. Offering her hand, she introduced herself.

"Your sister needs all the sleep she can get. She has only been able to sleep fitfully, a few minutes at a time. That's why I cautioned your parents not to waken her."

"How long has she been asleep?"

"Oh maybe ten, fifteen minutes."

"I'll have mom and dad go to the cafeteria. They plan to eat dinner there."

"Good idea. Thanks." The nurse gave Nora a 'just between us' wink and Nora motioned for her parents to join her in the hall.

"You're sure you won't come along, honey?" Nell urged.

"Positive, Mom. I want to stay with Bonnie. I couldn't eat anything anyway."

Nora sat quietly. She had a hard time dealing with the fact that it was really her sister lying there in that bed, her sister, Bonnie. She had just talked to her, maybe a week ago. Now she was here, so ill, so weak, so completely dependent.After an interminable amount of time Bonnie began to stir. She awakened gradually. Then suddenly she moaned with pain and clutched her stomach.

Nora leapt out of her chair and leaned over her sister, taking one of her hands in her own.

Bonnie's eyes flashed open in an instant. "Nore, oh Norie, thanks for coming. Thank God."

"Are you having labor pains Bonnie? Should I get the nurse?"

"What the hell for? They won't do anything about it." Bonnie's eyes slid to the door, then looked back at Nora. "Mom and Dad?"

"They went down to the cafeteria to eat. You were asleep."

"Good," Bonnie nodded weakly. She reached for Nora and pulled her close. "If I don't get out of this Nora, I want you to promise me, promise me you'll raise the kids. Not adopt them, or anything, they're Rick's kids, too. I just don't want his family to raise them. He's gone so much. They will, you know if you don't."

Nora began to protest. "Don't be dramatic Bonnie. I know you don't…"

But Bonnie cut her off. "Shh…don't argue with me. Just promise me, okay? I made a will last night. It's in my table, in the drawer." Bonnie waved a hand in the direction of the bedside table.

"All right! I promise! But shit! You're not going to die."

Bonnie smiled. "Just in case." Then she pulled Nora close again. "The baby is dead, Nore."

"What?"

"You heard me. The baby is dead. I know. It hasn't been moving at all. I've had two other kids, Nore. I know what it's supposed to feel like."

Nora began to cry. "I'm sorry. I'm sorry, honey."

"I know. I know you are." Bonnie was impatient.

"But then, when the Monsignor gets here and declares the fetus inviable, they'll remove it and you can come home. God, Bonnie, I'm so sorry. But there will be others. Plenty of others," Nora whispered.

Bonnie shook her head. "He was here. He was here this morning. Don't tell Mom and Dad. I don't know what they might do, especially Daddy. You know how anti-Catholic they are."

Nora wrinkled her brow. She didn't think her parents were anti-Catholic, or anti anything else for that matter. But that was beside the point. "What is it that you don't want me to tell Mom and Dad?"

"The Monsignor examined me along with my doctor, the head of the neonatal department and Sister Mary Briana. She's the head of the hospital. They were all here real early in the morning. They couldn't get a heartbeat but Monsignor said that didn't matter, the baby may have been turned over. I told him I haven't had any labor pains for the last two days, just these sharp pains in my abdomen. I'm not dilating. He smiled and said, 'Good, good. Maybe we can carry this baby to term.' He never once called it a fetus, always a baby." Bonnie's grip on Nora's sleeve tightened. "Nora, I know the baby is dead. Monsignor knows it, too. So does Sister Mary Briana and probably everyone else in this hospital."

"But what are you saying Bonnie? What would be the point?"

"The point is that they want me to carry this baby to term, dead or alive. Even it I have to stay in here to do it. They won't let me leave, Norie." Bonnie's fingers dug desperately into Nora's upper arm. "They'll never let me leave until my due date."

Nora had to control herself not to laugh. "But that's absurd, Bonnie. Like I said, what would be the point?"

"Honest to God, Nore? I don't know."

Their parents came back then and the subject was quickly changed. Nora chalked the whole thing up to drama. Bonnie had always had an active imagination. Maybe she was on some kind of medication, something that distorted reality a bit. One thing Nora knew to be true, hospitals were in the business of kicking you out too soon, if anything, certainly not of keeping you longer than needed.

Bonnie fell asleep about eight for a few minutes, and then again about nine-thirty. By then, Nora had really had it. It was decided that her dad would stay and her mom would take her home.

Zoey awakened to tiptoes and whispers. She smelled something, something unusual but wonderful, baby powder. She inhaled deeply and smiled, remembering where she was and who she was with. Laying on her right side, she moved her left arm to hold Ellie closer. At the same time she heard that loud, rasping whisper.

"Hi Grammy! Shhh! Be quiet. Ritchy and Aunt Zoey are asleep.

"Okay, sweetheart! You go back to sleep too," Grammy answered, covering the two of them up.

Then through the thin walls, Zoey heard continued whispering.

"Go on and go to sleep honey. You look beat. I'm going to read for a while, so before I turn in I'll come up and wake Zoey up to come to bed. Ellie will be sound asleep in a few minutes."

"Don't do that Mom. Zoey's fine where she is."

"Don't be silly, Nora. Ellie wiggles around like a worm on a hook, and in that tiny bed? Of course I'll wake her. It's no trouble."

"You don't need to do that Mom. Zoey's as exhausted as I am. We were up almost all night last night."

"All the more reason!" Nell's whisper was emphatic. "She needs her sleep!"

"Mom! Just leave her alone, for God's sake!" Nora couldn't take any more.

"Nora, if this is about you and Zoey, you don't need to be embarrassed, honey. Believe me, I'm fine with it. I don't want the two of you to behave any differently when you're here, than you do at home. I expect you to sleep together."

"But Mom. You don't understand. We're not really together," Nora began

"Oh, I understand more than you think I do," her mother cut her off. "You've just broken up with Gabriella and Zoey's probably just broken up with someone, too, and so you're cautious, taking it slowly. I think that's wise. But I was with you this afternoon, honey. I saw how things are between you. I can read between the lines. You two, after all these years, you belong together. I'm waking her up!"

"Mom, listen. Zoey slept in there on purpose, okay? You have misread the situation. We are not a couple. We could never go back to being one, not after the way she hurt me. That's for sure!"

"Oh, Nora," Nell said softly, and Zoey could tell by the accompanying squeaking spring that she sat down next to Nora on the bed. "Nothing is for sure. Don't you know that? Nothing in life is for sure. Look at your sister, the picture of health last week, racing around, shopping, volunteering at Ellie's preschool. And now..." Nell began to cry.

"Mom, I'm sorry. I didn't mean to..."

"It's okay. It's not your fault. It's just that you need to understand, Nora. Life is about taking chances. If you and Zoey aren't a couple, aren't together, then why the hell aren't you? Do you think time will simply stand still for the two of you? That you can sit back and deny your feelings in order to keep your hurt and anger alive? Can't you acknowledge those feelings and just trust them for a change? Tomorrow is not a guarantee, honey. We can't always just postpone life. We have to act on it today because that's all we really have for sure. You have to both want to do that and then just do it! Now, get in bed. We'll leave Zoey where she is if that's what you want."

Nora though about that for a long time. Long after her mother hugged and kissed her and went downstairs. Was her mother right? Did she and Zoey belong together? Was fate throwing them at each other these last few days for a reason? Should she take a chance here?"

Next door, Zoey was awake too. Once roused, she was unable to go back to sleep. Try as she might, she couldn't get comfortable enough to relax, let alone sleep. Sharing a bed with Ellie was less like sleeping with a wiggle worm and more like a windmill. She was just as apt to lie crosswise on the bed, as the more conventional pose, preferred by Zoey and the rest of the civilized world. Finally, after about an hour, Zoey decided to take her chances with Nora. A modicum of physical comfort was all she desired and, at that point, she just didn't give a shit about anything that anyone read into it. She was too wiped out to care.

17

"Nore, scooch over. Let me in."

Nora smiled in the dark. She was not asleep, but she pretended she was, grumbled a bit, and rolled from her left side onto her back.

Zoey slid under the covers, on her back, too. As she rolled onto her right side, the side she always slept on, she had the fleeting perception that she was on the wrong side of the bed. So what! She was too tired to care.

It was hours later before she cared. She awoke with a start, enveloped in another fragrance. A remembered scent, an essence of her essence. Fully awake, she realized Nora's hair had somehow fallen across her face. Before brushing it away, Zoey closed her eyes and allowed herself to breath deeply, and remember.

"Big deal," she told herself. "This is all Kings X. We can't be held responsible for what we do in our sleep." As she brushed away Nora's hair she was very aware of Nora's face. Lower in the bed than her own, and facing her. She came close to embracing her. Clasping that face to her breast, as she had earlier with Ellie. It would be easy, really. Then Nora's arm would go around her and, still asleep, their bodies would entwine as they used to.

There were only two impediments to this scenario. First of all, Zoey was not asleep and the therapist within her would not allow her to pretend that she was. Secondly, Zoey was sure that Nora really was asleep, which meant that she would be taking advantage of her. If awake, Zoey was certain that Nora would never allow anything to happen between them. Resigned, she rolled over, her back to temptation.

When Nora's arm did find it's way over Zoey's side, neither of them knew it. Nor were they aware of Zoey's firm grasp of that arm, and they never would have acknowledged either, they were both so soundly asleep. Never, except that they were made suddenly and rudely aware of these circumstances by an intruder.

In the very early hours of the morning Ellie awoke to find Zoey gone. She went potty and then went searching for her. She did not like where she found her and she did not like whom she found her with. She climbed up onto the bed and on her knees, next to Zoey, she yanked Nora's arm free of Zoey's grasp and pushed it back over Zoey's body.

"My Aunt Zoey," she admonished Nora crossly. Then she settled down in Zoey's arms. Soon Nora's arm was back, covering the two of them. This simply would not do. There were some things Ellie was prepared to share but Aunt Zoey was not one of them. Moving quickly and decisively, Ellie crawled up to the headboard of the bed, pulled herself upright, stepped over Zoey's head and, squatting, then sitting, she inserted herself one limb at a time between the two of them. Close to falling out of bed, Zoey rolled onto her right side, which fit right into Ellie's general scheme.

Nora's alarmed eyes flew open and locked on those of her tiny niece.

Once again Ellie informed her in no uncertain terms, "My Aunt Zoey".

"I brought her here," Nora teased, moving her hand slowly towards Zoey.

"No!" Ellie slapped at her hand. She glared at Nora. "I bite you," she threatened, her face as mean as she could make it.

"I'll tell," Nora countered.

"Who?"

"Grammy," Nora's smile was sly.

"Then I'll tell, too."

"But you would be telling a fib," Nora laughed. "I didn't bite you."

Ellie was on her knees again. "Hu! Uh!" she shook a finger in Nora's face. "I'll tell Grammy that you took my Aunt Zoey away from me. You took her out of my bed and put her in yours. And then, then you held on tight to her and wouldn't give her back."

"She's got you, Nore. Better give up while you still can!" Zoey's grin lit up the dawn.

"All right! All right! Don't bite me. You can have her! Now, lets all go back to sleep." Nora yawned and stretched. "I don't even want her, anyway," she had to add.

Ellie squinted her eyes up and looked at Nora for a long time. "Oh yes you do," she whispered.

"We rest our case," Zoey murmured, hugging Ellie to her.

Nora whispered something back, something about little brats and deserving each other as she rolled over, and almost off the bed. By six o'clock the three of them were in the kitchen, having given up on sleep. They had had cereal and toast and coffee and juice and were trying to be quiet and not wake up Grammy and Ritchy.

"I think I'll get dressed and go to the hospital, relieve Dad."

"Yes. It'd be a good idea to get there early. I'll go with you."

"You don't need to do that, Zoe! They might not even let you in to see her."

"If they don't, they don't. It'll do me good to get out, among the big people," Zoey shot her a desperate look.

By the time Nell got up and joined them in the kitchen, they were both dressed and anxious to get out of there.

Quick hugs and kisses were followed by a strict reminder. "You'll come back? Right after lunch? To take a nap with me?" Ellie whispered in Zoey's ear.

"I will, I promise."

She scowled at Nora. "You promise you'll give her back at nap time?" Nora hesitated, taken by surprise. "I'll tell. I'll tell Grammy!" Ellie knew a sore spot when she found one. She went straight for it.

"That little vixen," Nora fumed as they backed down the driveway. "If she tells Mom I stole you away from her and held you tight and wouldn't give you back, I swear, I'll…"

"Oh, Nore!" Zoey laughed. "She's a baby! Nobody is going to take what she says seriously. Although I must say, you have certainly had no trouble in sinking to her level."

"You don't understand. Mom and I had words last night about waking you up. About us sleeping together. I was embarrassed and she tried to reassure me that it was no big deal to her. So I had to tell her we weren't together. We weren't a couple."

"Oh," Zoey's eyes were enormous as she feigned ignorance. "And what did she say?"

"Nothing really. I know she didn't believe me, though. And now! If Ellie…if that little brat tells her…"

"Nora! Listen to yourself. Ellie isn't a little brat! She's a darling baby. She has spent the last year individuating and she is full to the brim with her own sense of self. I find it adorable, adorable and fascinating; staking out territory, stamping a foot, declaring ownership, mine! This is mine and you can't have it."

"But she has to learn. People are different. They don't belong to anyone."

"But they do Nore, to her they do. They are hers. Her mommy, her daddy, her brother…"

"And her Aunt Zoey," Nora broke in disgustingly.

"She's a little possessive right now. She'll get over it. Cut her some slack. This isn't an easy time for her, either. She knows something's wrong but she doesn't know what and nobody will tell her. I'm a temporary distraction for her. Just let it be. It's not hurting anything."

"You're right. I need to keep reminding myself that the kid is harmless. She's only three."

"Exactly. Which reminds me, I haven't had a chance to tell you yet," Zoey cleared her throat, "Gabriella called last night but I didn't know it was her and she didn't know it was me. She asked me to please take a message and then she went into this long number about your mom calling her house with a message for you about a medical emergency involving your sister. She went on to say that she had been trying to call you and didn't know where you were. She didn't want your mom to think she just blew off that message. She asked me to please tell your mom that she would keep trying to get in touch with you. So I told her she didn't have to do that. I said, 'Nora's here. She came today.' And that started Ellie chanting. 'Auntie Nora came today…' over and over. I was trying to shush her up and Gabriella was going off on how grateful she was and how worried she had been and Ellie, well, she got tired of me talking on the phone, I guess. She wanted me all to herself, probably, so before I knew what was happening, she tried to grab the phone out of my hand and she said it into the receiver."

"She said IT?"

"Yes. As loud and as perfectly enunciated as possible."

"My Aunt Zoey?" She said that? She said that to Brie?" Nora exploded.

Zoey bobbed her head up and down quickly. "By the time I wrestled the phone away from her, Gabriella had hung up. Either that or we disconnected her when we fought over the phone."

"God Damn it! What was it I said about a harmless three-year-old? That kid is the bad seed!"

"She's at a very literal age Nore. You know, you brought this on yourself. You said to her you did bring her something, remember? You said you didn't bring her a present, but you did bring her something, an Aunt. In her mind, I'm like a super, deluxe stuffed animal. 'My Aunt Zoey,' she said, and we all thought it was cute, but we didn't correct her. So, that's what I am to her."

"But Brie! Shit! God knows what she thinks. I guess I have to call her and explain."

"I think you should call her. Tell her what's going on with your sister. You owe her that. And she has been worried. I don't think you need to explain about me. What's to explain? Besides you don't owe her that. You are out of there, Nore. Do I have to keep reminding you?"

They pulled into the hospital parking lot. Nora parked the car and turned off the engine but made no move to get out of the car.

"I need to tell you something before we go in there, Zoe. Before we see Bonnie, or Dad. I need to tell you what Bonnie told me last night when we were alone. She says the baby is dead."

"Oh, Nore. I'm sorry. Why does she think that?"

"She doesn't think it Zoe, she knows it. She says the Monsignor adviser-guy knows it and her doctor knows it and the head of the hospital, Sister Mary Briana, knows it too. It sounds crazy but it has been bugging me and, well since you're here I wanted to bounce it off you. Besides sounding too crazy, I can't think of one good reason why they wouldn't acknowledge the baby's death, if it really is dead. Bonnie says they want her to carry it full term."

"That doesn't wash Nore. The fetus won't change if it's not alive. You're right. There's no compelling reason. Without a reason..." Zoey shrugged. "Maybe she has been on Demerol for a couple of days."

They walked into the hospital. "You go on up and relieve your dad. I'm going to the ladies room. Then I'll either be in the cafeteria, the chapel, or up with you," Zoey said as they parted. At Nora's questioning look, she elaborated. "The Chapel is the best kept secret in hospitals. It's quiet, nobody bothers you. A good place to think, or nap, if one is tired enough to nap sitting up." Zoey winked and grinned that grin.

She was that tired and decided to visit the Chapel first. If she was lucky, she would have a nice little nap and then get a cup of coffee. She peaked into the Chapel from the door. Actually, there were two doors into this chapel. Zoey was at a side door. To her left was a small altar with a stained glass window behind it. Rows of pews were directly in front of her and extended to her right – where the other door stood. On either side of that door, the chapel continued, storage closets on the right and smaller pews, long enough for two or three people, on the left.

"Perfect!" Zoey thought. She took a seat in the corner in the last row where she could lean back against both walls, in case she really did drop off. She closed her eyes and began deep breathing exercises. With each exhalation of breath, she felt some tension leave her body.

Zoey wanted to clear her mind. God knows there was a lot to clear; her parents, her sister, Kirsten, career decisions, and…and Ellie, damnit. Might as well think the unthinkable. At thirty-eight Zoey had thought she had left the baby thing behind a long time ago. She and Kirsten had never even considered children. Never even discussed it. There was no room in Zoey's life for a child, but then, Ellie. Just holding her, Zoey was filled with such yearning, such longing. It took her by surprise, knocked her off her pins, and she was unprepared. It's not that she was unhappy, miserable, or anything. And she had a wonderful full life, didn't she? Then why this, this visceral desire? For that's what this was, Zoey knew. Oh she knew all about biological clocks and a woman's hormonal urge to procreate and she thought she had dealt with all that. She had, hadn't she? This was something else, something different entirely. This was profound, puzzling and profound. All because of Nora. Wait, wait a second. Where did that come from? Well, it was Nora's fault to begin with, the way she presented her to Ellie. And, of course, if she hadn't come home with Nora she would have never even seen Ellie and she wouldn't be feeling this way. No, without Nora and Ellie, she would not be feeling this way. What about with Nora and without Ellie? No, never. Or with Ellie and without Nora?" Zoey couldn't even imagine that.

Was there something else going on here? They were very alike, the two of them. And Zoey had been just as tickled watching Nora relating to Ellie at her own level, as she had been with Ellie herself. Did she just want a baby or was Nora somehow even more involved? That thought so completely freaked her out that she was unable to finish it.

Zoey knew it would not disappear though. Better just to let it percolate there, on the back burner, along with her sister and cousin Willy. She would get around to that, too. All in due time. The therapist within her would have it no other way.

18

Zoey had been asleep about twenty minutes when she heard a rustling sound, an almost inaudible, "Oh, my!" and then a little louder whisper, "Excuse me!"

"Please, don't leave. There's plenty of room for both of us," Zoey said to the back of the retreating woman.

"I'm not leaving. Just going down to the next row."

In the dim light Zoey saw her whole face break into a smile, "So I can lean against the wall, too."

Zoey grinned back at her. *I bet I have her regular place,* she thought, closing her eyes again. Before she could go back to sleep, a teenage girl entered the chapel. She looked at Zoey and raised her eyebrows, "Dr. Hennessey?" she whispered. Zoey nodded. "Nora Fairchild gave me a message for you. She said to tell you she has taken her dad home and will be back as soon as she can."

"Thanks. Will you tell Nora when she returns that I'll be in the cafeteria if I'm not in with Bonnie."

Zoey stood to leave with the messenger, and was surprised when the woman in front of her did the same.

Once they were out of the chapel the other woman extended her hand. "Dr. Hennessey, sorry, I couldn't help but overhear. I should have known. Only a doctor would be tired enough to sleep sitting up straight like that."

"That sounds like the voice of experience," Zoey grinned. "I'm afraid I took your regular place."

"You did. I'll admit it. I'm Dr. McCoy. Welcome to St. Mary's. I know you're not a regular here. Assisting? Consulting?"

"Consulting, I guess you could say."

Leading the way, Dr. McCoy said, "Come on, I'll buy you a cup of coffee."

It wasn't until they got their coffee and sat at a table that Zoey and Dr. McCoy had a chance to really look at each other. And when they did, a stunned silence was followed by a gasp of recognition. "Zoey?"

"Bernie?" Followed by several, "Oh, my God's" and "I don't believe it's."

"But what are you doing here?"

"I work here, Zoey, have for three years. I swear, I would know you anywhere. You haven't changed a bit since graduation from St. Joseph's Academy."

"And you! I always knew you'd be a doctor. But how did you end up way out here?" Zoey could not believe it.

"Oh, you know, one thing leads to another. I ended up at Johns Hopkins. After my residency I stayed there, until I came here."

"You left Johns Hopkins to come out here?" Zoey's eyes were huge.

"Well, I'm a nun, Zoey. I have to answer my calling, go where I'm needed."

"What?" Zoey could not have been more amazed. "You? A Nun? Third Degree Bern? Why you could lie your way out of anything and on to the Dean's list! A nun?" Zoey flashed her a gleeful grin.

"Hard to believe, I know. But my dad got the bargain of a lifetime. Married me off and got free tuition to medical school in the bargain, plus all those years for surgery. At times I thought it would last through my eternal commitment. But what about you? I couldn't help but hear Nora Fairchild's name. Are you with her?"

Zoey nodded. "You know Nora?"

"No. Heaven's no." Bernie seemed flustered. "I know of her. Know who she is. Nora's caused quite a sensation around here. Her sister had a baby here year before last. Then her dad was here last year. Everybody makes an excuse to gawk at her. She is just the most beautiful creature and she's totally unaware of it, natural and unaffected. Is she really like that? Really as unpretentious and nice as she seems?"

"Yes," Zoey nodded, smiling. "She really is unaware of her effect on others and yes, I guess I'd have to say that she is that nice, although I'm probably not the best person to answer that."

"Sorry. Forgive me. I didn't mean to put you on the spot. You probably don't even know her that well."

"That's not what I meant, Bernie. And yes, I do know her that well," Zoey sighed. "Nora's my…my ex."

Now it was Bernie's turn to be dumbfounded. After staring at Zoey for a long moment Bernie nodded. "I always thought you were gay."

"Then you were always right," Zoey joked. "I always thought you were, too."

"Gaydar…takes one to know one," Bernie stirred her coffee. "I couldn't go there, Zoe, just couldn't. God wouldn't let me. My life isn't so bad. It's pretty much the same as yours I bet; close bonds of friendship; the fellowship of common goals, enjoying each other's company. Just no sex."

Zoey nodded. "Sounds just like my current relationship!"

"Oh Zoey, never change! You and your zany zingers!"

"Yes! Well it would be funny if it wasn't so true," Zoey muttered ruefully.

"Well, I would hope, at our age, that sex is less important than, say, commitment, trust, or that wonderful feeling of sharing, knowing all about someone and loving them for all that you know. Knowing too, that you'll never be alone. They'll always be there for you."

"Sounds good to me! Where can I sign up?"

"Tell me about you becoming a doctor, and what you're doing here."

"I didn't mean to mislead you back at the chapel. Just didn't want to get into it. I'm not a medical doctor," Zoey handed Bernie her card. "I'm a Ph.D., private practice."

"Aha," Bernie examined the card. "A therapist! How like you Zoey! But are you seeing a patient of ours?"

"It's just social, Bern. I'm just here with Nora."

"Oh, I see. You've remained friends although you're not involved with each other anymore."

"No, not really friends. It's a long story. She just broke up with someone. We went out to dinner to talk about it. She felt terrible. She took me home and we stayed up late, got into the wine. She spent the night in the guest room," Zoey added quickly at Bernie's expression. "Then my car was in the shop, so Nora took me to a local seminar I was attending, picked me up at noon. Then I went with her to get some of her things from where she had been living and took them over to where she was moving to. She took me to pick up my car. It still wasn't ready so instead we went to the market. When we got back to my house, things got a little crazy. Both of our partners were very upset that we had spent time with each other. I don't think Nora cares all that much. She was out of that relationship anyway. But I was ticked at Kirsten for not trusting me and for getting so angry. So, I told Nora I was planning to go to White Lake over the weekend to get our cabin ready for some friends my sister was entertaining next weekend. Nora said, 'Let's go, right now' and so we did. Got there about ten. I built a fire and didn't open the flue. Filled the cabin with smoke and we spent the night sitting outside on the porch. The next morning we had to clean the whole place and then Nora had this message from her sister, Bonnie. She was scared, crying and in such pain. Nora tried calling everywhere. She didn't know where Bonnie was or who her doctor was. So we got here yesterday and drove from White Lake. I had probably only seen Nora four maybe five times in the last four years until Wednesday night. So you see, there's nothing really between us. We're not even exactly friends."

Bernie began to laugh. "And you're a shrink?"

"Meaning what?"

"I may be pushing forty, Zoey. And I may be a nun. But I'm not so naïve, or unworldly, that I believe that one! What a crock!"

"But it's true, Bernie. It happened exactly the way I told you."

"And you, my dear, are so full of it! Would you know true love if it came up and bit you on the butt?" She waved off Zoey's protest. "How about true love seeking your advice after a breakup, or carting you around to and from a seminar. Letting you tag along, picking up and dropping off personal things; how about true love doing your marketing with you. Did she come home and put the groceries away, too?" Bernie teased. Zoey nodded uncomfortably. "And then going up to clean your family's cabin? Who would do that Zoe? Who in the world would want to do that? True love, that's who. The same true love who would drive all this way. You couldn't let her come alone, could you, Zoe?"

Zoey said nothing. She shook her head, admitting something to herself at the same time that she admitted it to Bernie.

"Well, the good thing is, you're here, and Nora's here for her sister."

Zoey noticed a sudden stillness in the cafeteria. It was as if everyone in the cafeteria line was playing that kid's game, Freeze, and all eyes were directed towards the entrance. Zoey grinned, glancing in that direction. "Looks like Nora is here!" She waved as she said it, and Nora, smiling at everyone, made her way to their table.

Zoey handled the introductions. "Nora, this is Bernie, Bernadette McCoy. She's a surgeon on staff here. We ran into each other in the Chapel. We were in the same class at Saint Joseph's Academy."

"For wayward girls," Bernie added under her breath. "Can I get you some coffee? Zoey, another cup?" they both nodded.

"So, how's it going? Your dad holding up?"

"He's fine. Slept like a baby. Bonnie said every time she woke up he was sound asleep. I think he mostly wanted to go home and shower and watch his games on TV."

Bernie returned with a tray carrying their coffee.

"I've been back for a while," Nora continued, "but they kicked me out of Bonnie's room. They're giving her a bath, changing her bed, doing the floors."

"All those hospital routines," Bernie threw in.

"Yes, and it's not even nine in the morning." Nora checked her watch. "I'm glad I found you Zoe. I need you to come with me up to Bonnie's room. I want you to hear what she has to say. It sounds crazy, but I believe her." She gave Zoey a look and then nervously glanced in Bernie's direction. "I'm sorry to get into this in your presence, you being on staff here, but this doesn't concern you, doesn't involve surgery." Nora leaned forward her forearms on the table, and whispered, "I'd just like to know who in hell is in charge around here!"

"Uh, well, that would concern me, I guess." Bernie pointed to her chest. "I don't know about hell, if we have anyone in charge there or not, but everywhere else, it's me!"

Nora and Zoey sat with their mouth's open, blown away completely. Nora finally recovered enough to speak. "You? You're Sister Mary Briana?"

Bernie nodded.

"Breeawna?" Zoey dragged out the pronunciation with sarcasm.

"What can I say. I was only a kid. Twenty. I read it in a novel. Thought it sounded dramatic and sacred at the same time. I don't know now," Bernie shrugged. "So go ahead, my dear. Why would you like to know who is in charge?"

Nora gave Zoey a look. Then she took a deep breath and revealed everything her sister had told her.

Sister Mary Briana was attentive. More than attentive, her eyes never left Nora's.

"And so," Nora finished, "even though Bonnie has had two other children and I believe she knows what she's talking about, I can't imagine a reason for any of it."

"Oh, well, I can give you one reason, or a big part of the reason, Monsignor Rovaldi," Sister Mary Briana said. "You see, you don't request Monsignor's opinion and then, after the fact, overrule it. If he says the fetus is viable, then it is a baby and to be treated as such."

"But that doesn't make any sense," Zoey argued. "Are you telling me you agree with his opinion?"

"I don't agree or disagree, Zoe. That's not my job. And I did not send for Monsignor Rovaldi, I might add. That was Dr. O'Connor's doing."

"And you wish he had not been sent for?" Zoey looked at her knowingly.

"You got it! The guy's a self-absorbed, holier-than-thou prima donna! But you didn't hear it from me."

"And he has a lot of influence in the hierarchy?" Zoey guessed.

"He is the hierarchy! Their direct representative, at least. It's a numbers thing too. I won't lie to you." Sister Briana looked from one to the other. "We're dependent on that very hierarchy for funding. We compete with all the institutions of learning, as well as the hospitals. We live and die by our stats here."

"So, what you're saying," Nora spoke slowly, "you're telling me my sister's right but there's nothing you can do about it!"

Sister Briana looked around her. Her voice was low when she spoke. "I'd prefer to put it another way. Perhaps it's not my place to do something about it."

Zoey hit the table with her fist in frustration. "Bernie! Would you stop talking to us like a Jesuit Priest. Give me a common sense secular explanation of what is going on here."

Bernie glared at Zoey. She bit her lower lip. "Still the same Zoe. Hell, or high water you won't take no. Bonnie was beginning to go into labor when Dr. O'Connor checked her in. At twenty, twenty-one weeks it's common practice for us to terminate labor, to give the baby a better chance to survive. She had some edema, a little headache, but nothing dramatic. I was concerned that she was possibly pre-eclampsic but Dr. O'Connor said this was her third child and she had similar edema with the other two pregnancies. Then her blood pressure shot up and stayed up. That's when Dr. O'Connor called for Monsignor Rovaldi."

Nora shook her head. "Why? I don't understand this."

"Because," Bernie lowered her chin and her voice, "delivery is the treatment of choice for pre-eclampsia but Dr. O'Connor didn't want to take the responsibility for delivering a baby that premature."

"He was just passing the buck." Zoey slammed her mug of coffee down on the table and then dabbed with a paper napkin at the mess she had made.

"Well Zoe, a Catholic doctor, a Catholic patient, a Catholic teaching hospital, cut him some slack. He was just trying to do the right thing. Anyway, as soon as the Monsignor came on board it was a totally different ball game. He said the baby was viable, so be it!" Bernie clenched her teeth bitterly.

"But Bonnie said they couldn't find a heart beat and she's sure the baby is dead. It hasn't moved for days."

Nora wiped her sweaty palms on her pants and her eyes welled up with tears.

"The official notes of the examination reflect that Monsignor detected no abnormal fetal heart pattern."

"But you could do an ultrasound and prove failure of fetal growth," Zoey thought aloud.

"True, I could, and I could appeal Monsignor's opinion. Been there, done that. It doesn't do any good. Even if I win, I lose, money wise," Bernie shrugged.

"But if the baby is dead, Bern, what do you get out of prolonging the inevitable." Zoey really was puzzled.

"I get weeks Zoe, same as Dr. O'Connor and Monsignor Rovaldi and Bishop Donnely and the Cardinal. If Bonnie can carry the fetus to twenty-eight weeks, we're all home free. We can even induce and, statistics wise, the baby, through act of God, is stillborn."

Nora and Zoey were both appalled. Nora spoke first. "But Bonnie says she's in pain and they won't give her anything for it."

"Her pain is epigastric, in the stomach. Doctor doesn't want to give her anything that might damage the fetus."

Zoey hit the fan there and then. "Bullshit, Bern! The fetus is beyond damaging! It's dead, damn it!"

Sister Mary Briana regarded them both calmly. "Bonnie told the Monsignor that she is no longer having labor pains. That is true and will remain true as long as she is my patient, but it's a free country. Check her out of the hospital. Take her over to Riverside General. They can perform a very simple procedure, one that I can't allow here, now, and your sister will be home tomorrow and back to normal very quickly."

Zoey leaned over and kissed Sister Briana on the cheek. "Thanks Bernie," she said, tears in her eyes. "I know that couldn't have been easy."

"Well you're wrong on that account at least. It's always easy for me to follow the Lord's will; when I've been paying attention and know what it is anyway."

Zoey gave her a funny look...questioning.

"You don't think for a moment that we met this morning by pure happenstance, do you? And that you accidentally came all this way with Nora? Just for no reason? Tune in and turn on, as we used to say." Sister Briana stood up. "Come on, let's go to my office. I'll get the discharge papers going and you can call over to Riverside. Tell them to expect you."

Thirty minutes later, Zoey and Bernie were still in her office. Nora had gone up to bring Bonnie downstairs.

"You might as well cool your heels here. You have at least a half hour before they'll appear."

"Thanks again, Bern. Even though I don't have a dime invested, I'm still so grateful."

"Well, it's like I said, the Lord works in mysterious ways. But are you teasing me or testing me Zoe?" At Zoey's non-comprehension she continued. "Well, I'm not an expert on love, as you can imagine. I've never even made love."

"Really Bern? Never ever?"

"Nope. Just like the olive oil. One hundred percent virgin," Bernie held her left hand in the air. "You are looking at the real McCoy!"

"Probably the only one for miles around," Zoey laughed.

"At least I don't know what I'm missing. I have been in love, though. A long time ago, Gloria Van Volian."

"No! Second Story Glory? You're kidding! She snuck in late every damn night. There wasn't a window that girl couldn't worm her way through."

"I was usually unlocking them and holding them open for her. Our relationship was doomed from the start, sexual orientation wise."

"True! She was the poster girl for Boy Crazy."

"Oh, and she used to tell me all about them; who was the best kisser, who she was craziest about. It drove me mad with envy and desire. But it was all in my head."

"I wonder what ever happened to her. She would have made an excellent cat burglar. She was so adept at leaping around on roofs and balconies, window ledges and parapets."

"I don't know. Lost track of her after graduation. But I still remember that feeling, that glorious, miserable, loving, hating that you love, feeling. I've been reminiscing, bathing in the vibes, since you and Nora joined me this morning."

Zoey regarded her sharply. "Too much water under that bridge, Bernie.

Even if that was what I wanted, Nora would never, ever come back to me. She couldn't ever forgive me for what I did to her."

Bernie looked at her with eyes that saw it all, eyes that knew everything. Well, after all, that was her job. "I'll pray for you Zoey," she said as Zoey left her office.

19

Zoey pulled up to the hospital entrance just as Nora came out of the door, accompanied by several orderlies and a nurse pushing Bonnie in a wheelchair. Zoey shook her head in amusement as Nora, unaware of adulation as usual, ran to open the car doors.

"Did they give you any trouble?" Zoey asked Bonnie, who got in the front seat next to her.

"Au contraire! They were glad to see us go. Didn't you think so Nore?"

"Well, relieved at least," Nora jumped into the backseat, slamming the door hard. "But I still feel like we're escaping from jail."

"You aren't the only one! I swear to God, when they brought me those discharge papers to sign and I saw Sister Mary Briana's signature, and then the admittance fax from Riverside, at first I thought you'd faked it somehow, Nore. I really did! Where is that stuff?" Bonnie shuffled through some papers. "Oh, here it is. There's an envelope for you Zoey. Dr. Hennessey from Dr. McCoy: 'Patient's Records,' it says."

Zoey took the envelope and tossed it on the dash. "You want to go anywhere? Do anything? Or do you want to go right there?"

"I want to get to Riverside as soon as I can. The doctor I talked to scheduled an exam at eleven to start the IV drip. They'll do the procedure before three so I can be released tomorrow noon." Bonnie began to cry. "God, I'll be glad to get this over with."

"Me too," Nora patted Bonnie on the shoulder. "We'll grieve later, and there will be more babies, Bonnie. You know there'll be more."

"I know," Bonnie closed her eyes. "I know Norie. This is not the end of the world. This is a fetus, a stillborn fetus under three and a half pounds and it is not, damn it, viable!"

The three of them shed silent tears; in unison, and yet very separately, each lost in very private thought.

At Riverside General, the last thing Bonnie said to Nora as they wheeled her down the hall on a gurney was: "After you tell Mom and Dad what happened, I need to have you explain to Ellie, Nore. I need to have her know before I come home tomorrow, that I won't be bringing a baby."

"Don't worry. I'll explain. Auntie Nora will explain it all."

"You guys will hang out with me tomorrow at mom and dad's for a while, won't you?"

"Sure, for a while. I'll have to ask Zoey when she needs to get back."

Nora ran to the car and got behind the wheel. "Sorry! I didn't think it would take that long."

"Don't be silly. Don't give it a thought." Zoey had spent the time reading and re-reading the missive from Bernie, but she certainly was not inclined to mention it to Nora.

After a beginning paragraph devoted to her joy at their reconnection and her hope that they would stay in contact, Bernie had written, "It was a fair and cloudless day, when the fair and lovely Miss Fairchild joined us for coffee. Was there ever a child with a fairer name? I wish we had eaten something. I would be most interested to know if she deemed our fare to be good or just fair and is the fare, fair...price-wise? I can't think of another word in the English language that is more complex and fraught with nuance, the exact opposite of Nora herself. She seems so simple, clear and steadfast. I will pray for her to love you in that exact way: simply, clearly and steadfastly, not because you asked me to, but because I know God wants me to. God and I together can be real pushy! For the Love of Glory, Bernie."

Ellie met them at the door and, firmly grasping Zoey by the hand, led them into the kitchen where Grammy and Papa sat at the kitchen table.

Zoey shot Nora a fleeting smile, tickled at the scowl darkening her features.

Over lunch Nora explained the morning's occurrences.

"Well Zoey, aren't you amazed that Sister Mary Briana turned out to be your old school friend?" Nell wondered.

Zoey favored them all with her spotlight grin. "Not as amazed as I am that my old school friend turned out to be Sister Mary Briana! Believe me! She was so full of the devil! The last person you would imagine would end up a nun."

"Well, whatever! I'm grateful to her for standing up to all those bozos that make the church's rules!" Wade growled.

"I got the impression, Dad, that it wasn't the Church's policy, as much as it was Monsignor Rovaldi's policy."

"That's what I thought, too," Zoey concurred. "Bernie wanted to help. She really did. She did what she could, the only way she could."

"Come here Pumpkin. Auntie Nora wants to talk to you." Nora scooped Ellie up onto her lap. She wiped jelly off her face with a napkin and kissed her on the nose. "Guess what? Mommy's coming home from the hospital tomorrow." Ellie squealed with delight. "But, remember how Mommy said she was going to get you a baby, and she would get it pretty soon after it was your birthday?"

Ellie regarded her with a serious expression, knowing somehow that something was coming. "Well, it turns out she won't be getting a baby after all. She went to the hospital early, to try and get one, but she couldn't get it this time. She'll have to wait for a while and maybe try again."

Ellie saw her Grammy wipe a tear from her eye. She looked at Nora. "Is Mommy sad?"

"Maybe…maybe just a little sad sometimes, but not too sad. She's happy too, because she has you and Ritchy."

Ellie nodded her head and smiled sweetly. After a moment's deliberation she decided, "When she gets sad she could have My Aunt Zoey. If," she added, touching foreheads with Nora, "she gives her back!"

"So, we are right back where we left off this morning," Nora frowned.

"If you all will excuse me," Zoey stood up, "I am just exhausted. Ready for our nap?" she asked Ellie, before things got ugly.

Nora decided to rack out, too, and her mom and dad were anxious to get to the hospital. "You girls are on your own for dinner. Help yourself to anything. We'll eat at the hospital," her mom said.

"I hope the food's better at this one," her dad added.

Nora turned the machine on to answer only and the telephone ringer off, so as not to disturb her two – no, make that three – sleeping babies. Then she took her cell phone and stretched out on her parents' bed and called her sister.

Bonnie answered on the first ring. "Hey! They let you have a phone already?"

"Sure, no problem. They're so cool here. I'm in a private room. I may not even go into labor or delivery. I've just had a few pains and I'm dilating already. It's, it's so tiny, Nore. And after two kids, it's no problem. I'm so relieved to be here. Everyone has been so kind, so understanding. I finally talked to Rick, too."

"Oh, good, how is he?"

"Okay. Mostly scared about me. You know how he is. If I'm okay with it, then so is he. I acted okay so he is too. He's going to try to shorten the trip. Try to get home a week from today. He could leave now, on an emergency, but I told him not to. Then he'd have to go back to finish up and it would take even longer. I just don't know how long I can hack it at mom and dad's. They mean well, but they spoil the kids rotten."

I read you loud and clear, Nora thought. "They're on the way over as we speak. Have somebody call me when you're, uh, when it's over," she said aloud.

Then she started to call Sybil. No, she thought, that would be really unkind. Brie doesn't deserve to hear all this from Sybil. Resolutely, she punched in Gabriella's cell. Let's see Saturday at one-thirty. She's out of the gym and is either on her way to meet someone for lunch, or she's at lunch, or she's had something to eat at the gym and is still there having a massage.

"Hello."

"Hi! You in the car?"

"I am, as a matter of fact. On my way to meet Roni and her Hollywood contingent for a late lunch." Gabriella had her cold, hard, what can-I-do-for-you, attorney voice going.

"Zoey told me you called."

"Yes, I enjoyed the humiliation of that, as I'm sure you can imagine. Baring my soul, how I'd been trying to reach you. I even lost it, started to cry. She must have had a good laugh. Probably was with you the whole time I was tearing my hair out."

"It wasn't like that Brie," Nora said, tiredly. "Didn't Sybil tell you? I asked her to tell you."

"Of course she told me. Could hardly wait to tell me that Zoey had an emergency. And you had to take her and because of that you had to turn your phone off for the whole night. The whole night! Jesus, Nora, you didn't expect that to fly did you? I mean, with Sybil, maybe, but God!"

Nora let her rant on and on and on. "Besides, that was Thursday. This is Saturday in case you hadn't noticed. Gee, what's missing here? Oh, I know, Friday."

"We went to White Lake, Zoey's family has a cabin, and we ended up going there to spend the night."

"Don't tell me. Let's see, you went there because it was so much closer, after Zoey's emergency, than coming home. And it had nothing to do with moonlight on the lake, stars in the sky, the two of you enjoying romance by candlelight."

Nora laughed. She couldn't help it. "Well, you're right about the candlelight, at least." Then she told Gabriella in detail about their romantic night. "Truly, it was a test of our sanity, our ability to cope. Then the next day, after we cleaned the whole place, we were just about to crash, we were so wiped, I called for messages and there was this really awful one from Bonnie. She was so scared, and I got so scared. I couldn't reach anyone. Didn't know where Bonnie was, who her doctor was. Thank God for Zoey. We just put our stuff in the car and Zoey drove all the way down to the interstate. We got here about four-thirty. That night I went to the hospital with mom and dad and Zoey took care of the kids. That's when you called. Zoey didn't know who you were."

Nora proceeded to tell her about Bonnie's condition and what she had told Nora when they were alone.

"The next morning Zoey and I went early to the hospital. Thank God I had her with me. I never could have gotten Bonnie out of there without Zoey."

Before Nora had a chance to thoroughly explain, Gabriella had done a one-eighty. 'See, that's what I always tell you, Nora. You're too damn nice. You hold back. Don't want to make waves. Sometimes you have to stand up for what you believe. Make a big stink. Good for Zoey. I'm glad she was there, too. If you had called me, I would have had their Holy Roman asses in court before they could have recited an Our Father."

Nora let that slide on by. "So, things happened fast, Brie. We got her into Riverside General. Took her right over there this morning. Mom and Dad are there now. This is the first chance I've had to call anyone. Bonnie'll be here tomorrow and I guess we'll be home tomorrow night, maybe Monday."

"I'm sorry, Nora, sorry I got so upset. I totally misunderstood the situation. I'm glad Zoey was there to take care of things, and to be there for you, too. I'm just," Gabriella sighed, "I'm just jealous. Sorry it isn't me there, to comfort you."

"I know," Nora whispered, suddenly unable to talk.

"Take care Nora. Take care of yourself. Get some rest, okay?"

"I will. I am. I'm going to conk out right now, as soon as I hang up."

Nora heard a change in Gabriella's tone. "And Zoey? Where is Zoey?"

"At the moment, Zoey is upstairs taking a nap with her new best friend, my niece Ellie."

"Well, tell her," Nora could sense the relief now, "tell her I'm sorry I hung up on her."

Nora got off the phone. Was it her fault that Gabriella jumped to conclusions? That she jabbered and interrupted so mercilessly that Nora couldn't get a word in edgewise to explain? She began rationalizing with animal anecdotes: let sleeping dogs lie; never look a gift horse in the mouth; a bird in the hand…and a bee lies sleeping in the palm of my hand.

She fell asleep smiling and slept the sleep of the righteous until she was awakened by the ringing of her cell phone. "Hello," she answered.

"Where the hell do ya talk? I don't see where you talk into."

"Hi, Dad. I'm here!"

"This part? This flip-flap? I thought that's what you held to your ear."

"Dad! Hi! I'm here!" Nora said louder.

"God damn foreign junk. You can bet this wasn't made in the US of A."

Then Nora heard her mother's voice. "Someone's on the line, Wade. Here, give it to me. Hello."

"Hello," Nora laughed.

"Hello Nora? Nora Fairchild?"

"Yes Mom. Mom Fairchild, It's me."

"Well what luck! It's Nora, Wade."

"Mom. It isn't luck. Dad dialed my number!" Nora's patience was wearing thin.

"I know, dear. But he didn't know, really, what he was doing. Bonnie gave us her cell phone to bring home. I swear! That man! Give him any kind of machine, and…"

"Mom, how's Bonnie?"

"Well, that's why I'm calling. They're all finished. She'll be back in her room about five and Dad and I are going to have dinner in there with her. Isn't that nice? I'm sure she'll call you herself then. Is everything all right there?"

"Just fine Mom."

"Well, good. We won't be late. I want to get up early and get everything sparkly clean before Bonnie comes home."

"Okay, Mom. See you whenever."

Zoey and Nora spent the rest of the afternoon cleaning and straightening up the house so Nell wouldn't have to do it.

"You know, now that I'm getting the hang of it, I might just hire myself out when we get home. It'd sure be a lot simpler than what I do now," Zoey wiped the perspiration off her brow. "Want the windows and the screens done? That's the weekend special!"

Nora swatted her on the rear as she passed by.

Zoey and Ellie picked flowers from the garden while Nora gave Ritchy an early bath. She wanted to bathe both of the kids early so she could scrub the bathtub, as well as the rest of the bathroom.

"I don't want to have my bath yet. It's too early. Then you'll make me go to bed early." Ellie accused Nora.

"No I won't. Don't be silly," Nora took off Ellie's shoes and socks. "You couldn't go to bed now anyway, even if you wanted to. Your sheets and Ritchy's are in the washer."

"Why?"

"So they'll be nice and clean." Nora tested the tub water and turned it off.

"Are you gonna wash your sheets too?" Ellie allowed herself to be further undressed.

"I am. But not until tomorrow morning, so they'll be nice and clean for Mommy when she comes home."

Ellie climbed into the tub, a big smile on her face. "Mommy will sleep in your bed and Aunt Zoey will sleep in mine."

Shit! Nora thought. Aloud, she explained, "Aunt Zoey and I have to leave tomorrow Ellie. "We have to go home, we have to go to work. Don't cry sweetie. You know Auntie Nora never stays here. How can I come back? How can I come see you if I'm already here?"

"But My Aunt Zoey. I thought she was different. I thought she was mine. And that she would stay."

"Well, she is yours, your very own Aunt Zoey. She isn't anyone else's Aunt Zoey. But that doesn't mean she can stay with you for always. What would Mommy think about that? Or Daddy. I don't think they would like that very much."

Ellie thought about it. "I could keep her here, at Grammy and Papa's."

"That wouldn't work. Grammy wouldn't want Aunt Zoey to stay here all the time. A visit is one thing but Grammy and Papa like to be alone together, too."

"Uh, uh, I heard Grammy tell Papa that she's never been as happy to see anyone walk through her door in her whole life as she was to see Zoey."

Nora frowned. "But she meant for a visit not forever. Besides, Aunt Zoey has her own place. She's busy, like I am. And she has friends, lots of friends. And she wants to be with them too."

A tear rolled down Ellie's cheek, but she was beginning to understand, Nora thought.

"Does she take a nap every day? Or, only 'cause she's here with me?"

"I think it's only because she's here," Nora whispered.

"That's what I thought. Mommy told me adults don't need to take naps," Ellie whispered back. "But I didn't know because Aunt Zoey goes to sleep so fast, always before I do. Does she go to sleep like that before you do, too?"

"Well, honey, Aunt Zoey and I don't sleep together. We have our own beds, our own places."

Ellie was wide eyed. "But, but I saw you."

"But that's just because there weren't enough beds here for each one of us to have one. We would both rather sleep alone than with somebody else."

"Uh, uh, " Ellie was insistent. "Not Aunt Zoey. She would be lonesome all by herself. She hugs me real close and holds me tight. That's how I know. Doesn't she ever hug you when you have to sleep with her because there's not enough beds?"

"I don't know, maybe. I guess. Come on, let's get you dry now."

Out of the tub, and wrapped in a towel, Ellie whispered in Nora's ear. "When she hugs you like that she means she's glad you're there with her and that she's not all by herself."

She's only three…she's only three. Nora kept repeating to herself all the way down the stairs.

20

Zoey was out on the screened porch with Ritchy. He was just tall enough to see out the screens and into the back yard and was busy watching birds fly in and out of an old pine tree, thankfully for Zoey.

"My God! I'm exhausted, just following him around. I finally brought him out here. With the door closed, he's at least confined and within sight! Is it five o'clock yet?"

"It is somewhere, as dad would say. What do you want?" Nora went into the kitchen to check the inventory. "Vodka?"

"Sure."

"With?"

"Not picky at this point, Nore. Just about anything. Anything but bouillon." Zoey referred to a night best forgotten, but still remembered; They were caught in a thunder storm at a horse show, and ended up in a makeshift tent, shivering and wet and drinking 'bull shots' They were miserable but too stupid to know it.

Nora returned with two stemmed glasses. "Noratini's," she smiled handing one to Zoey.

Zoey took a sip, "Excellent! The flavor is good but, um, unidentifiable."

Nora waived a hand in dismissal. "Grapefruit juice, honey, salsa and um, pickle juice."

Zoey's eyes narrowed, "No shit?"

"I almost went for the bouillon, honest to God, but I didn't want anything hot. It's just vodka and water and a little Tabasco."

"Hits the spot. I don't know when I've ever been so tired, really down deep tired to the bone. Maybe that's why this tastes so great. You just made it up?"

"Not really. It's Gabriella's drink of choice. I called her this afternoon, like you said."

"Nora, please. Don't say that. You called her, period. It certainly wasn't because I said to. Or, at least I hope it wasn't."

"Right! I only meant that you told me she called. I returned her call."

"And?"

"And, everything's cool. She said to tell you she was sorry she hung up on you and she told me she was glad you were here with me."

"Nora? What did you tell her?"

"Only the truth. About Bonnie, and switching hospitals, and how I never could have done it without you!"

Zoey grinned that grin and took another sip of her drink.

For dinner they had the much-traveled swordfish with applesauce and macaroni and cheese, left over from Ellie and Ritchy's dinner. "An innovative combination, but all-American, comfort food," Zoey decided.

Nora picked up Ritchy ready to put him down for the night, but Zoey held out her arms. "Let me hold him Nore. After chasing him around this afternoon, all wild and crazy. I want to feel what he feels like now, mellow and ready for bed." Zoey took Ritchy and his bottle and sat in the maple rocking chair. Her elbow fit perfectly on the arm of the chair and Ritchy's head fit perfectly in the crook of her arm. She rocked slightly as she held his bottle. He held it too, at first, but then was content to allow her to support it while he merely caressed it. Soon, he was caressing Zoey, too, her arms, hands and breasts. Zoey felt herself fill with deep and profound emotion, and she knew that her feelings earlier that day, had not been an aberration. She was not done with the baby thing, not by a long shot.

Meanwhile, Nora had been reading to Ellie. "But I just read this. This too. You pick a book and let Auntie Nora read the whole thing to you. I don't like reading just one page."

"Aunt Zoey does. She likes my best pages."

"Well, Aunt Zoey has her hands full at the moment." They both looked at Zoey holding and feeding Ritchy.

Ellie did not like what she saw. "He's ready for bed and so am I."

"You are? Without a story?"

"Oh, my Aunt Zoey will read me a story when we're in bed."

"No. I'll read you a story if you like, before you go to bed. Then Aunt Zoey and I will go to bed later."

"It would be better if she went to bed when I did," Ellie confided. "She always goes to sleep first. And she's real tired, Auntie Nora. Remember? She said so earlier."

Nora and Zoey exchanged a look and a smile. "Aunt Zoey is not sleeping with you tonight, Pumpkin. She's sleeping with me."

Ellie got angry. "But that's mean! You don't want to sleep with her. You even said you didn't. You don't want her to hug you and hold you tight! And because you want to sleep all by yourself, you say that Aunt Zoey does, too. And she doesn't. And I don't either. I like it when she hugs me. You should let her sleep with me if she wants to. If she doesn't want to be alone."

Zoey had stopped rocking Ritchy and she was giving Nora that 'over the non-existent reading glasses' look that she had perfected.

"You, uh, just had to be there," Nora explained hastily.

"Let's all go up to bed," Zoey said quietly, pointing to Ritchy, who was sound asleep.

During harsh negotiations between Nora and Ellie, Zoey got in bed, the double bed, this time on the right side so she could lay on her right side and face out. After three Noratini's she didn't care where anyone else slept.

It was finally decided that because Aunt Zoey was not moving, and because Auntie Nora was not sleeping in the twin bed in with Ritchy, that all three of them would sleep in the double bed for the first half of the night, from seven-thirty until nine. After that Ellie would sleep in her own bed for the second half of the night.

By the time the kid knows better, she won't remember tonight. Nora smiled cunningly as she and Ellie quietly crawled into bed with Zoey. Ellie put her finger over her mouth as she slid over Zoey's inert form, over to the good side, where Zoey's arms enfolded her and held her tight.

Nora found herself sleepily watching the clock on the bedside table. It was only eight-thirty. How could she possibly be so sleepy? Ellie was right. Zoey zonked out first, as soon as her head hit the pillow. She was really exhausted. It wasn't much longer before Nora knew by her breathing that Ellie had gone to sleep too. Then, looking at the clock, she had a sudden realization. *Duh! Ellie can't tell time. What the hell is the matter with me?* She got out of bed, lifted Ellie from Zoey's arms and tucked her in her own bed. Then she went back to bed. Zoey had rolled over onto her back and was smack in the middle of the bed.

For no reason, other than to avoid the green glow of the bedside clock, she told herself, Nora got in on the right side of the bed, in the exact same spot, still warm, where Ellie had been.

Predictably, it wasn't long before Zoey rolled back onto her right side. Her arm went, automatically around Nora. Was she awake? Nora didn't think so. Still, she grasped Zoey's hand in hers and wound her arm around Zoey's. Why? Just because she felt like it, damn it.

Sometime later, Nora rolled over and she and Zoey faced each other, their bodies in a full-length embrace.

That is how Nell found them at ten o'clock when she came upstairs to check on the kids and turn the hall light off. She smiled and shook her head.

The next morning found everyone up early and bustling around. In spite of Nora and Zoey's efforts of the evening before, there was still plenty to do. By ten o'clock, Nell was off to the market, Nora and Zoey went to Riverside General to pick up Bonnie, and Wade was left in charge of the children.

"Don't let them get dirty again, Wade," his wife cautioned from the front door.

He waived her off. "No. Wouldn't want their mother to see them dirty, for God's sake," he grumped.

Nell got home first, in time to get the chickens in the oven to roast, and the potatoes going, before the other three returned.

Bonnie, though frail and pale, had washed her hair that morning and it shone like copper in the sun. Her mom, watching from the kitchen window, cried with relief and gratitude when she saw her get out of Nora's car. She cried again when Bonnie embraced her dad at the front door. He lifted her off the ground in a bear hug the way he always greeted his baby girl.

Zoey, the last one in the door, held the screen back, and held herself back, too, not wanting to intrude on the intimacy of the moment. She watched intently though; watched Bonnie's face when the kids came racing in from the other room; and when Bonnie lost it, Zoey lost it, too.

Nora, who was standing behind her sister, turned around to look at Zoey, to see if she had heard what she thought she heard. She had. Zoey was a mess.

"What the hell?" Nora was surprised. She went back out to the front porch with Zoey, "You okay?"

Zoey just shook her head crying openly.

"But Zoe…what…what is it?"

"I just…I just…when I saw Bonnie…when she saw the kids…" Zoey couldn't tell her.

But by then, Zoey didn't have to tell her. "It's not the baby thing again is it?" Nora whispered, amazed.

Zoey nodded. "I thought until I got here, I was over all that, I really did. But Ellie is so sweet...and then Ritchy...he just finished me off."

Nora stared at her. *This is really too weird,* she thought. "Well, it's an emotional moment, Zoe. You're just caught up in it, and tired."

"I slept from eight until six this morning, Nora, that's ten hours." Zoey went into the kitchen and splashed cold water on her face.

Bonnie and her mom sat at the kitchen table and Zoey joined them. "Just like I said on the phone this morning, it was a breeze. The people couldn't have been nicer. It's kind of hazy. They must have given me something. They explained what they were doing, but it didn't register. This morning Dr. Mann asked me if I had any questions and I said, 'No.' I really don't want to know, you know?" Bonnie looked at Zoey and her mom who both voiced agreement.

Ellie and Nora came to join them in the kitchen. "Ritchy doesn't really like baseball. He just likes sitting with Papa in Papa's chair and he likes Papa's pretzels."

"And how do you know that?" Nora wondered.

"Cause he never watches baseball at home. He doesn't know what it really is. He's only a baby."

Nora raised her eyebrows. "Then why does he cheer like that?"

"Just cause Papa cheers and he hears the people cheer on TV and he likes to yell loud like that," Ellie shrugged.

Nora pulled out a chair next to Zoey but before she could sit, Ellie climbed onto it. Nora pulled out another chair.

"Ellie, you get down. That's Auntie Nora's chair. You sit over there!" Bonnie ordered.

Ellie wiggled around but didn't get down. "I don't want to."

"Then come and sit on Mommy's lap."

"No! I want to sit here by My Aunt Zoey!"

"Mommy didn't ask you what you wanted to do Ellie. I said, get down and let Auntie Nora sit in that chair."

Nora started to sit. "That's okay, no big deal."

"No, Nora. It is not okay, Ellie." Bonnie fixed her with an, 'I mean business' look, "You get down and come over her right this minute."

Eyes on the ground and mouth in a pout, Ellie complied with orders.

Bonnie lifted her up to her lap. She raised her chin so she and Ellie were looking at each other. "That was rude. Aunt Nora pulled that chair out to sit in it and you jumped right up and took it. That's not nice."

"But I wanted to sit there."

"But Aunt Nora wanted to sit there, too."

"No she didn't. She just didn't want me to sit there. She didn't want me to sit next to Aunt Zoey, to My Aunt Zoey!" Ellie turned and glared at Nora.

"Eleanor O'Reily you apologize to your Aunt Nora this minute. And then I want you to go in and play with Papa and Ritchy. The adults are having their own time in the kitchen!"

Ellie looked right at Nora when she apologized, but it wasn't over yet. They both knew that.

"Dear God, that child!" Bonnie exhaled noisily. "She is a constant challenge! I used to laugh at Rick's brother. Whenever you asked him how the kids were, he'd say, 'If they were six feet tall we'd have to kill 'em.' I'm beginning to see what he meant."

"Well, she's been an absolute angel since she has been here. Such a help with Ritchy," Nell put in.

"Right. Too much of a help. She totally dominates him. He'll never talk as long as Ellie is right there every second of the day to speak for him. In fact, that's one of the main reasons for this one." Bonnie touched her stomach. Then, as the ice water of reality hit her in the face, her voice trailed off. "I mean...that was... was..."

Nell took her in her arms. "Let it go, let it go darling," she said, through her own tears.

Zoey lunged for the kitchen sink and the cold water. *What is wrong with me? What's happening to me,* she thought desperately.

"It's the getting used to it that's so hard," Bonnie said quietly. "You know, another baby. I had a plan. Now everything's different. I have to accept it, I guess."

Nora wrinkled her nose. "I don't think it's about 'accepting.' It's nothing deep. You just haven't realized it completely, that's all. It's still new, Bonnie."

From where she stood Zoey could look past the kitchen table into the hall leading to the family room. She saw Ellie holding Ritchy's hand, helping him to walk. The sweetness of the scene overwhelmed her, bringing more tears. But, then, as she watched, she saw Ellie steer him into the hall, whisper something to him and let go of his hand. Ritchy dropped to all fours and scrambled into the kitchen calling out 'Mommy...Mommy,' just as Zoey suspected his sister had instructed.

Bonnie picked him up and held him on her lap. There's Mommy's big boy! You're getting so big! Did you miss Mommy?"

Then Ellie made her entrance. "Ritchy! Ritchy! Come back in here. The adults don't want us to bother them. Leave Mommy alone, even if you do miss her."

The four women looked at each other and rolled their eyes.

"Come and sit on Aunt Zoey's lap for a minute you manipulative little monster," Zoey laughed. "Now, when it's time for you to get down, I want you to find those books we had before, the ones Ritchy likes, and I want you to lay on the floor with him and read those books to him. Point to the pictures while you read them, like you did for me. We want to make sure Ritchy understands the stories."

"Bravo." Nora clapped as Ellie and Ritchy left the room. "Especially impressive, as Ellie doesn't know how to read."

Zoey grinned that sudden, spotlight grin. "True, but at her age, she's too young to realize it! Rather like telling time."

Nora's face suddenly turned beet red, "She was awake. Rolled over to see what time it was. Shit, she was awake when I got in bed on her side. Wait a minute here. Then she was awake when she rolled back onto her side, I bet, and when she put her arm around me!" Nora gazed speculatively at Zoey, trying to decide. Were you? Did you?

Zoey's eyes danced in merriment. Wouldn't you like to know, they said.

The women spent the remainder of the afternoon in the kitchen, occasionally preparing something for the early Sunday supper, but mostly chatting.

"So, tell me Zoey, how you happened to come all this way with my sister?" Bonnie had asked. This began a recounting of the entire saga, beginning at dinner last Wednesday. They all laughed about the sequence of misconceptions, especially about Gabriella and Kirsten getting so pissed at them. And by the time they got to the smoke filled cabin, and Dillen, and Lillian, they had become quite raucous.

Dinner followed pleasantly enough and afterwards, still sitting at the dinner table, Zoey held Ritchy one last time. She felt the baby skin on his cheek and inhaled that baby powder scent.

Then she held Ellie, who patted her hair and face again, committing it to memory. "You'll come back."

"Of course! Of course I will."

"But you'll still be my Aunt Zoey, even before you come back, even while you're gone away."

"That's right, sweetheart. I'll still be your Aunt Zoey and I will miss you very much when I'm gone."

Satisfied, Ellie traded Zoey's lap for Nora's "Did you hear her?" Ellie's eyes were huge. "She's My Aunt Zoey. Even when she's gone away."

Nora nodded. "I heard."

"You promise you'll bring her back?"

"I promise, Pumpkin. I'll bring her back," Nora smiled around the table.

"Did you hear the other? That she will miss me?"

"I did. And you know what? I'm going to miss you, too."

"No you won't, not like My Aunt Zoey will. Not at bedtime, when we hug and kiss. That's when she'll miss me. Would...would you sleep with her sometimes? I know you don't want to."

"Ellie!" Bonnie was horrified, but there was no stopping Ellie, not yet.

"I know you like to sleep by yourself, but she doesn't. She'll be so lonesome and sad." As if things weren't bad enough, Ellie began to cry.

Nora stood up and carried her into the family room She cried some too, and she whispered, "I'll try, okay? I'll try to sleep with her and hug her and hold her tight, okay?" Nora pulled back a little to see Ellie's face. "If you ever tell anyone, Mommy or Grammy or anyone, I swear, I will bite you!"

Then Ellie giggled and Nora, wiping away both of their tears, began to tickle her. The trauma passed them by.

Good-byes, put off until the very last minute, were hasty when the time finally came. And, at seven sharp, Nora backed out of the driveway. With many big waves and two small toots, they were on their way.

21

They spent the first few minutes straightening the front seat and the dash; finding the bottle of water; recharging the cell phone; cleaning dark glasses; adjusting the air and finding mellow music on the stereo.

Nora sighed, "Well, back to reality. Back to the real world."

"Is that how you see it? I was just thinking the opposite. Sort of back from the real world."

"What's that about!"

"Only that these last four days have been so totally different from my everyday existence and yet, so much more real. I guess I mean physically real; smoke in the damn cabin, exhaustion from sleep deprivation, losing a baby…real, trying, difficult, emotional situations. A slice of life. I don't know. It makes my own life seem so cerebral."

"Well, duh! I mean that is what you do, Zoe. You don't fix people's broken bones. You fix their insides."

"Yes and I think it's harder for me to relate to my patients' pain, loss and frustration because my training's all about handling it. Getting past it and through it and dealing with it. I never know how I'm doing. I have no method of measuring success or failure except for what my patients tell me. They're happy, they can deal now. Thank you, goodbye. But I never really know. Have I made any real progress? Are they really in a better place? Or have I merely taught them how to suppress, how to compensate and project."

"Oh, Zoey. Stay out of that quagmire. It's a no-win situation. You just get in deeper and deeper."

"Believe me, I know that. I was just explaining. It's not like scrubbing screens."

"Or like being pregnant and losing the baby," Nora whispered.

"No, not like that at all."

Nora looked at her apprehensively.

"It's okay. I'm all right. I'm not going to cry again, at least not right now." Zoey put her feet up on the dashboard, knees bent in front of her chest, arms on her knees.

"You could though. You could go off at any time if you gave yourself permission," Nora said, knowingly.

"Maybe," Zoey sighed and closed her eyes.

"I can't believe it's the 'baby thing' still, or is it again. I thought you were so beyond that. You were over that way before we broke up."

"I know," Zoey sniffed. She opened her eyes again and there were tears in them. "I thought so, too. Honestly it was just, I guess it was just those kids. Ritchy is so precious, so trusting and dependent. And he responds to having his simplest needs met. He's so happy to get his pants changed, or to eat his num-nums and he's so loving, in such a pure sense."

"And Ellie? I thought Bonnie was going to have some kind of attack when Ellie asked me if I would please sleep with you. Talk about a mortifying moment!" Nora laughed merrily.

Zoey grinned at her. "You were a tad upset yourself, as I recall. It serves you right though. Never confide in one who does not share your own sense of right and wrong, even if it is due to a lack of maturity."

"Confide! You think I confided in that little demon? That was all from inside her own head."

"Well someone told her you would rather not sleep with me."

"But that was only because she accused me of stealing you away from her and keeping you for myself!"

Zoey's laugh was like a bell ringing. "Oh, I adore her! She is simply delicious! She's at my very favorite age! You both are," she added, tickled with herself.

Nora's brow furrowed. "I don't see what's so damn delicious."

"It's her own little personality. She's developing her own personality. It's fascinating, and at the same time, so endearing."

"Yeah, well maybe you think so. I think if her little personality keeps developing the way it has been, she'll be a possessive, jealous, scheming little brat."

"She's supposed to be like that Nora. That's where she is, developmentally. Although, I must reiterate that you certainly have no trouble relating to her on her level. What did you say to her when you took her into the other room? Whatever it was, it certainly did the trick. She seemed fine after that."

"I told her a secret."

"Oh, yeah? What was it?"

"It was a secret, between the two of us. I can't tell you."

"You might as well," Zoey giggled. "Children that age are incapable of keeping secrets. I could call her right now and find out, I bet."

"Oh, I don't think so," Nora replied mysteriously.

"You seem confident."

"I told her if she told anyone…anyone…I would bite her."

Zoey laughed uproariously. "You're there, Nore, at my absolutely favorite age!" She reached over and squeezed Nora's cheeks with one hand.

"But am I fascinating and endearing?"

"Rather," Zoey thought about it, "in a possessive, jealous, scheming sort of way." Impulsively, she reached for Nora's right hand and gave it a squeeze. "She's very much like you, Nore. That's probably why I'm such a sucker for her."

"Right! You were always such a sucker in our relationship."

"Maybe I could have been. If you would have let me be. I always had to take the tiller. Be in charge. Call the shots. But there was a time, in the beginning, when I was so crazy mad for you. I was a sucker then."

"Yeah, and then the 'baby thing' hit you." Nora shook her head, remembering. "Just out of the blue. You just…One day you were fine. The next day you just went bananas, crying every time you saw a baby…a baby anything."

"Well, it was hormonal, I guess. I was young, and in love, and…" Zoey's feet hit the floor and her left hand flew to her mouth. She stared, unseeing, out the passenger window of the car and they drove on in silence.

Whatever it was that stopped Zoey in mid-sentence, Nora just did not want to know. The silence became awkward. Nora weakened. Finally she compromised. "It's not an uncommon thing Zoe, a woman wanting a baby. What do you say to your patients?"

"You know. The regular. It's so selfish. How can you care for a child when you have to work? The 'gay' issue. Is the ridicule fair to the child?…bla, bla, bla." Zoey sounded grim. "It usually works. They get a puppy or something."

"Well…"

"Well, I don't want a puppy, Nora! It's different than a 'want' anyway. It's not like any other 'want' in my life. It's a desperate ache...an acute dread."

"A dread Zoey? Come on!"

"It's true. I dread the life ahead of me," Zoey admitted. "I am full of such regret now. I can't even imagine what it will be like in ten more years, in twenty years. I'm afraid if I remain childless, it will just snowball and I'll be miserable."

Nora pulled over to the shoulder of the interstate. "No shit, Zoe?" she was stunned.

Zoey turned to face her. "Ellie was right, I loved sleeping with her. I loved holding her against me, feeling her heart beat."

Nora looked at her and smirked. "The intimacy for free; no maintenance, no relationship."

"It's hardly the same thing. But I admit you're partly right. I do miss the physical presence of another person. I don't really like sleeping alone. Ellie was right about that, too."

"She was right about me being jealous, too, the little bugger." Nora drove back on to the highway.

"Of course she was, Nora. That was her whole, snotty, little, rub-your-nose-in-it plan, to make you jealous! What's the fun in having your very own Aunt Zoey if you can't lord it over the other kids!"

"You want to stop at E.Z.? Last chance before we cross the state line."

"I don't know. What for?"

"Well, to stock up. Brie usually gets wine...you have to buy a case, but there's no state tax."

Zoey shrugged, "Why not."

They bought a case of wine, some beef jerky because Nora felt like she needed something hard to chew on, and a couple of Cokes, which got promptly spilled by a joint effort. Zoey set them temporarily on the personal console while she fastened her seat belt and Nora, watching the traffic from the driver's side window, pulled suddenly out onto the road. Zoey cleaned up Coke for the next ten miles.

"That just about does it for up here, at least." Zoey looked at the pile of tissues on the floor. "I hope you don't want any water. I used it all."

"I'm fine, still have ice." Nora rattled her cup and stuck it between her legs. Their stop delayed them a little and it was almost ten thirty by the time they pulled into Zoey's driveway. They completely unloaded Nora's car in order to clean up the spilled Coke in the back seat.

"Put all your stuff in here." Zoey dropped the unused sleeping bags on the dining table. "Tomorrow you can hang some clothes in the garage, in those garment bags if you want to."

"You're sure Zoey? Sure that will be all right?"

"I don't see why not. It's only temporary. Those bags might as well stay in my garage as in Sibyl's," Zoey shrugged.

"Okay. Then I'll just get my cosmetics bag and I'll see you in the morning."

"Our bag," Zoey corrected her. "All my stuff is in there, too. Look Nore, just stay here tonight. It's too late to go all the way to Sibyl's and I don't feel like sorting through everything. Tomorrow we can go through everything together. Get organized."

That made total sense to Nora. "Thanks Zoe. I'm bushed." She looked at Zoey who was eyeing her answering machine pugnaciously.

"I really do not want to deal with this," she sighed and rewound.

Nora went into the kitchen and returned with a glass of wine for each of them. Zoey fast-forwarded through her sister's message that she had heard at the Lake.

The next one was from Kirsten. "Damn it Zoe. I don't know if you are really out at this hour, it's almost ten-thirty, or if you are in there, hiding in the dark. At the moment I don't care. I refuse to stand on your front porch and bang on the door and I left my keys at home, so that's where I'm going should you care to call me there. It's obvious that, as you would say, we need to talk."

The next message was from Polly. She would not be there until ten but would stay later in the afternoon to make up for it. "What do you bet the Yankees were on the tube?" Zoey smiled.

The next, a message from Joan. "Hi Zoe, just wanted to tell you Dad's much better. Don't worry. It's about eight here. Mom's on her way into the city and I'm off to work. Talk to you later."

Then Zig from the Jaguar place. 'Sooee, I am zo zorry, Sooee. But my two bezt men are out today. There iz no one I truzt to work on your car today. I know I promised you and I feel zo bad. Call me Monday and rent yourzelf anything you want. I will pay the cozt!'

"Uh, Dr. Hennessey? Marj from the agency. Lorraine had to leave early for Ft. Lauderdale so she can't keep her eleven o'clock,' Zoey raised a fist in the air. All Right! My only appointment for the day!

And then Kirsten…again. "This isn't a phone call. I'm sitting here at your desk, speaking directly into your machine. I have spoken with Sybil, as well as with Gabriella and so I know of your emergency house call. You neglected to mention the location of the house, however. It must have been far, far away. It's almost ten and Polly arrived just when I did. I'm meeting Gabriella for lunch after that I take my mother to the doctor. Then we have a meeting this afternoon. Call me when you get this message. I'm worried about you, Zoe. Worried about us."

Elbows on her desk, Zoey closed her eyes and rested her head on her fingertips.

"Zoey…Zoey, hey! It's Cole Templeton. Just called to touch base. Your name came up at a faculty meeting yesterday. I…uh, mentioned that we had talked. The response was enthusiastic, as I knew it would be. Don't think I'm rushing you, pressuring you. I don't mean to be. It's just that your name did come up and I thought I'd give you a call. Talk to you later."

Nora raised her eyebrows in question. Later, Zoey mouthed as they heard Kirsten's voice once again. This time she was clearly upset. "It's me again. I stopped by after my meeting with Gabriella. I couldn't believe you would just go off somewhere without letting me know. It's so unlike you. I know your car is in the shop and I theorized that your cell phone is in it as it is turned off. Your service hasn't heard from you and neither have I. I know you left with Nora but couldn't imagine that you would still be with her. I usually don't think about foul play. I don't know if it's paranoia, or if it's spending time with Gabriella. She has worked herself up into an emotional derangement over Nora. But the more I sympathize with her, or try to comfort her, the more distraught I become. Anyway, I came back this afternoon because this is so unlike you. I came looking for a clue, a message." Zoey raised her face to the ceiling, squeezed her eyes shut and waited. A silence of close to thirty seconds followed before Kirsten could go on. "I got it…got the message," Kirsten began to choke up, "loud and clear. Nora's clothes hanging in the closet, more in the dresser drawers, her prescription in the medicine cabinet…her luggage. I noticed this morning that only the bed in the master bedroom was unmade but nothing registered then. I didn't know then that Nora had spent Wednesday night here. I don't need to ask you what happened, Zoey, or even how it happened. Only why." Kirsten's voice was barely audible as her last words turned into a moaning sob. "Why did you do it this way, you of all people. You couldn't tell me? Face to face?" Tears ran down Zoey's face.

Nora hit the stop button and pulled Zoey from her chair into her arms. The embrace was comforting, not amorous. Meant to console, not to convey passion.

"God, Nore. She's in such pain!" Zoey whispered, in pain herself.

"I know, I know," Nora stroked her hair, whispering too. "But it's not your fault Zoey. Kirsten, and Brie, too, have just made a big deal over such an innocent thing. We haven't done anything. Before, what I did with Alison, was unconscionable. But you had nothing to do with that. And you and I...well there is no you and I."

Nora could feel her coming back. She moved her arms, then put them around Nora and gave her a squeeze. She took a deep breath and exhaled slowly. "You're right. I didn't do anything. And still, I caused her so much pain. That's the worst part about it. Kirsten's right. It's so not like me to just go off like that. That's where the betrayal occurred. I betrayed our commitment to each other by doing that. I was furious with her and it doesn't matter what happened or didn't happen. It would almost be better if something had happened. At least it would be better than, 'I just didn't give a shit.'"

Nora finished her wine. "Sounds like we're back again at the conversation of Wednesday night – using someone to break up with someone else," she held their empty glasses up.

Zoey nodded and wiped away tears. "Should I call her? Call her right now?"

Nora shook her head, thinking about it. "Probably not. Then you'd either have to say I was here, or lie."

Zoey nodded glumly. "I need another hug."

They hugged each other like sisters and Nora went off to fill their wineglasses. When she returned, she held her glass up in the air.

"Zoe, this weekend, every minute of it...I'd do it again in a heart beat. No matter what happens, I want you to know I enjoyed just being with you. I'm glad we did it."

Zoey just looked at her. "So am I," she said slowly as they clinked glasses.

22

They listened to four straight calls from Zoey's service, three new patients and one returning for a so-called 'tune up.' Nora went to retrieve a chair from the dining room and she heard Zoey make a phone call.

"Cole, I know you won't hear this until tomorrow sometime, but I've just returned from out of town. Just received your message. You've given me a lot to think about. Dissolving my practice is a huge step for me. Still, I'm excited at the prospect you have offered and wanted to let you know. We'll talk soon."

Nora sat next to her. "What's going on Zoe?"

"Cole Templeton, you heard his message earlier? Well, he has asked me to join the faculty at the University. Teaching, diagnosing and teaching diagnosis, post grad. It's a tempting offer, more money and much, much less stress. I've been considering it for a couple of weeks. Trying to decide what to do. Looking at it from a purely altruistic viewpoint, which is what I always try to do, I should probably stay in private practice. After all those years of school, hundreds of hours of continuing education and supervision, I finally feel confidant that I can help my patients. Really make a contribution." Zoey looked at Nora and shrugged. "On the other hand, the longer I continue to see patients, and the more I hear the same things over and over, the harder it is for me to think of each patient as an individual, as unique. They just aren't to me. Not anymore. Maybe you should get out when you start to feel like that."

Zoey faced her desk and went on. "We came home and I came in here, sat at my desk and looked at the answering machine going crazy, flashing all its lights. That's where the temptation comes in. That and the feeling that I can't continue to go through what I go through every day and come out unscathed without also becoming hard, judgmental, unfeeling and non-caring. I feel myself turning into that, and I don't want to. I don't want to see people as robots. 'Oh God, here she goes again.' I've lost patience with my patients. But then I have to stack that up against the commitments I've made to those patients and the consequences of breaking those commitments, some of them would take it as a betrayal. It could mean a serious setback."

"It's a terrible responsibility." Nora nodded. "I don't know how you've stood it this long. In the car when you talked about how real these last few days have seemed, I thought it seemed that way because you were just Zoey and not Dr. Hennessey and you let yourself feel and respond. You felt the pain and worry and joy and love. And you didn't have to do anything with those feelings. You could afford the empathy."

"Yep! I sure can't afford it at work! In fact, it's been a long time since I let myself open up like that."

"Since the last time you got the 'baby thing.'" They eyed each other thoughtfully and Zoey turned on the machine again.

They winced, as Kirsten's voice seemed to fill the whole house. Zoey turned the volume down. "Oh Zoey, Zoe, Zoey. What can I say? I feel so wretched. I spoke with Gabriella and she told me she talked to Nora this afternoon. I should have known that if you went off somewhere you had a good reason. Doing good for someone, somewhere. It was kind of you to go up to the cabin to help out your sister. I confess that when I was at your place yesterday I listened to your messages. Well, I was looking for clues, and I heard the one from your sister, about your father. I'm so sorry, honey. Having all that on your mind and then all that dreadful Catholic business with Nora's sister. Thank goodness you were there. Gabriella felt badly that she got upset and hung up on you. She knows she should confine her anger to Nora and Miss Teenage California, but she can't help herself. She has such a temper. Goes into a jealous rage. Very, very Italian. I, on the other hand, being a Scandinavian brooder have been busy doing just that, brooding and feeling badly too. I felt badly that I didn't matter enough. I told myself to get a grip. How were you supposed to know I was coming home? You probably kept calling me at the cottage, and got no answer. But then I thought, no, Zoey didn't leave her house Thursday night sometime between seven, when I talked to her, and nine, when her sister left her a message, suddenly and without telling me, because she didn't know I was coming home. She did that because she did know. You found out I was coming and you left so you wouldn't have to face me. Face me and tell me what Zoe? What couldn't you face telling me? Never mind. You don't have to answer that. The question was purely rhetorical. I found the answer every where I looked yesterday, Nora has obviously moved in. I guess I could shrug it off. Tell myself that you two are just good friends, that I trust you. Until you tell me differently, I'll just figure you're letting her stay there until she finds a place. But how can I shrug it off Zoe when I recall the look on your face every time you see her? You try valiantly for a smile but it can't cover the pain in your eyes. How can I shrug it off when I remember you, remembering her, looking at a picture, or going to a certain place at the beach, or a certain restaurant? Your smile turns funny and I know I've lost you, momentarily, and you are back with her. How can I shrug it off, huh, when my whole life is going down the toilet?"

"Shit!" Zoey muttered at her machine. This was followed by an echo from Nora.

"Don't worry. I'll explain in the morning. She'll understand."

They heard the machine click and then a very familiar stage whisper. "I can do it. I can hold it myself." Then, in a louder voice, "Aunt Zoey, Mommy told me you won't get to your house for two or three more hours, but they're making me go to bed now. Mommy is in the kitchen with Papa and some friends and I told her I couldn't go to sleep until I called you, so Grammy said I could call you now and tell you a...a..."

"Message," they could hear Grammy prompting.

"Yes...a message. Well, It's about Pooh Bear. Papa got me this big one and he's brown and I'm gonna sleep with him tonight. And I have another one at home. He's not so big and he's yellower, but he's squishier, too. So I could send you one of them. Whichever one you want, to sleep with you so you won't be sad, if Auntie Nora won't sleep with you. I know she doesn't want to. She has never even once slept with me, even for a nap. I don't think she'll be so good at it, but she promised me she would try to hug you and hold you tight and sleep with you. But don't tell her I told you that or she will bite me. I think Pooh Bear might be better than Auntie Nora so tell me which one you want...what? Oh Mommy wants me to tell you to tell Auntie Nora that she can't wait to talk to her."

"Shit!" Nora said it again.

Zoey laughed her bell-pealing laugh. "Out of the mouths of babes," she chuckled.

"I only said that because she was crying," Nora explained desperately.

"But you really told her you would bite her? Seriously? I thought you were joking."

Nora made an exasperated, 'Uh' sound in her throat and shook her head quickly from side to side. "I didn't want her to tell Mom, for Christ's sake. Tell Mom or Bonnie that I promised her I'd try to sleep with you...Jesus!" Nora let her head fall back and slapped her hands over her face.

"Never mind that now. Nobody is going to make as big a deal out of it as you are. The important thing is, which one shall I choose, the bigger, browner one? Or, the littler one that's squishier...hhmmm?"

23

Nora lay in bed trying to rationalize her way back to lucidity. "There's no need to get so stressed out over something so trivial," she told herself. "After all, it's only my mother and my sister who both love me very much. And Zoey, who doesn't seem concerned in the least."

In fact, Nora could hear Zoey humming as she went about her nightly routine. Finally she heard her snap off the rest of the lights and get in bed. That's the last thing Nora heard. She didn't hear Zoey get up a couple of hours later. Didn't hear her come and sit on the edge of her bed. Didn't know she was there, or how long she had been there, until Zoey whispered her name.

"Nore? Nore…"

Nora rolled over, still asleep, and reached for her. She pulled her close, discovering her cheek was wet against Nora's own.

"I can't sleep, Nora. I'm sorry to awaken you, but I need to talk to you. I'm afraid if I wait until morning I'll convince myself of hundreds of reasons why I should not say what I need to say. I know you were upset about Ellie's phone call earlier and I completely made fun of you. I ridiculed you and disrespected your feelings. I had no right to do that just because I was amused, personally. It was terribly self-centered of me and very unfair. In fact, I haven't been very fair to you these last four days and I feel really rotten about it. Starting Wednesday night, I shouldn't have said what I said about you flirting and everybody hitting on you. I know better than that. I know you don't mean to do that. You can't help it. It's just because you're so damn beautiful," Zoey whispered in her ear.

"Oh, come on Zoe. I'm not that beautiful." Nora pushed her away so she could look at her in the moonlight streaming through the open window. "Besides, you heard what Sybil said that night about her bridge friends."

"But that's all because of the way you look, too, honey. Don't you see? Sybil would say the same thing about anyone who looked like you. And yes…you are that beautiful, and it's not your fault, and I should not have said what I did. You don't come off like that - flirting and frivolous. I can't let you think you do.

"At the hospital Bernie asked me about you. You seem to have caused quite a stir there, and you acted as though you were totally oblivious to it. She wanted to know if you were really like that and I told her that 'yes you really were.' I said it instantly, without even thinking about it. I knew so completely that it was true. That made me wonder, Nora. Made me doubt myself. Why did I say all that to you? I was projecting my own insecurities and jealousies, I'm afraid." Zoey sighed, looking down at her. "Forgive me?"

"There's nothing to forgive Zoe. You're my friend for Christ's sake. Wednesday night you were just trying to be a good friend and you felt that, as a friend, you needed to tell me that. Now tonight, after you've thought it over, you've changed your mind. Now you feel, still as my friend, that you need to tell me you were wrong. Fine! I appreciate it. Honest. I'm not sure that you were wrong the first time. Maybe I do flirt all the time."

"Well, if you do, you don't mean to. It's completely unconscious."

"How can you be so sure?"

"Because it has been happening to me, Nore. You flirt; lead me on, I go for it, come on to you, and you don't even realize it. I know you really don't. All that stuff about Ellie, to me it was fun. She is too cute and you are too cute with her. You totally turned me on. I loved every minute, flirted and teased. Pretended to be asleep. It was only after I got in bed tonight that I admitted it. And then I knew for sure that it was totally unconscious on your part. You weren't playing around. It was for real with you. You really did get down to Ellie's level and you meant it when you told her you didn't want to sleep with me. You were scared, Nore, scared of what might happen. I knew that, damn it! So, what did I do? I rolled over into the middle of the bed when you got up to put Ellie in her own bed. I…I was surprised you got in on the side you did," Zoey's voice dropped to a whisper. "But it wouldn't have mattered Nore. I would have gone for it, rolled either way. I couldn't help it, the need to touch you was so overpowering. I'm so, so sorry Nora."

"Hell, don't be such a shrink, Zoe. Don't you think I felt the same way? I mean, shit! The two of us in a double bed? What would you expect? It was no big deal. In fact, I liked it. Liked your arm around me. Of course I thought you were asleep."

"I know you did. I couldn't believe it. Then you actually went to sleep, too; incredible! That's when I began to realize how truly clueless you are. It's also when I realized something else."

Zoey sat up straight and her robe fell open, revealing that she had nothing on under it. Tears slowly made their way down her face and neck. "I can't be your friend, Nore. God knows I've tried, given it my best shot. But I...well, the truth is, I'm faking it. I'm nothing but a fraud. Lately, my whole life has been one big fraud and I...well, I can't continue the charade, now that I see the truth. You know what a 'thing' I have for the truth." Zoey stopped. Choked up, she began wringing her hands. After a minute she went on, "It's not that I've been lying to you, Nora. It's that I've been lying to myself; rationalizing, repressing, denying, compensating. I can't believe it. Can not believe the depth of my own self-deception. Now I need to deal with the consequences. I can't allow my self-deception to be the cause of your pain any longer. I just can't."

Fully awake now, Nora stared at Zoey. She was distraught, quivering all over, and when Nora reached for her and tried to comfort her, she pushed her away. "I have to do this, Nora...please...I have to."

"Okay," Nora held her hands up on either side of her face.

"I lied to you from the get go, beginning Wednesday night at dinner. I told you that I knew you were in pain and I didn't want to talk about my relationship with Kirsten because it wouldn't help you. That was partly true, but I didn't want to talk about Kirsten and me because I didn't want you to know what our relationship was like. It wasn't your pain that concerned me but my own."

"After dinner, when we were in your car, I said I was crying because it hurt me to see you hurting so. That wasn't true either. I didn't weep for you, but for myself. For us, or at least what used to be 'us.' I wept for the beautiful young lover I once had. You were exactly how you described Alison as being: full of awe and wonder and joy. You couldn't get enough of me, either. It hit me so sharply; the bitter, stinging reality of it. Then, later, listening to you describe how I ruined your life. It wasn't the first time you have told me that, but it's the first time it tore me up inside. I cried, Nore, because I had to own up. I had to acknowledge that you were right. I did it. It was all my fault.

All that bull I talked about that night...that's all it was...bull. I rationalized my way into accepting that pitzicaca crap for reasons to end what we had. It was easier to live with myself, I guess, if I could think I left you because of rotten or annoying things you did. Facing the truth about this is the hardest thing I've ever undertaken. But I have to be honest. I have to be, at least with myself. Oh, I was annoyed sometimes when you had people over without telling me ahead of time and I admit to being jealous of everyone you were with, and the band, I really did hate that band. I hated the music you made; irritating, repetitive drivel. But all of that wasn't really responsible for what I did. You wondered why we didn't get some therapy before I broke up with you. I have to say Nore, that one hurt. Hurt me deep inside. It just leveled me, honey. The problem that we had communicating was so big to me. So important, and so obviously a clear call for therapy. It forced me to admit that, at the time, I didn't want to save what we had." Zoey shook her head and shrugged, still crying.

"I met Kirsten and I just went insane over her. She enthralled me and bewitched me. I really was insane, I think, and completely obsessed by her. The way our relationship turned out, it would be a comfort to me if I could blame it partially on you and what was happening with us. But that would not be honest on my part. My code of honor demanded that I break up with you before I was unfaithful to you. So that's what I did."

Zoey had to stop then. She was crying too hard to go on.

"I know." Nora gave her hand a squeeze. "I guess I should thank you for that, at least."

But instead of comforting her, what Nora said had the opposite effect on Zoey. Rocking back and forth, her hands covering her face, she moaned, "Oh Nore! Oh God! Oh God, Nore!" over and over.

She still wouldn't let Nora touch her, so all she could do was watch in dismay until Zoey gained enough control to talk again. Then it came dribbling out, a little at a time, between the choking sobs and the moans.

"If only...if only I hadn't been so God damn honorable. If only Kirsten and I had made love...even once. I never would have left you. She...she told me she was lousy at full time, day to day relationships and that she was self-centered and that her work came first. I said 'fine' but I had no idea what that really meant. She insisted that we not live together. I thought, well, okay, she had such a weird schedule, and all. And I was so thoroughly, madly in love with her that I was willing to settle for anything, even just a fling. In my madness, I was willing to give up what you and I had for any relationship at all with Kirsten.

What I didn't realize was how cerebral she was, how much time would be devoted to the planning, talking about and then remembering the fling and how little time actually would be spent in the 'flinging.' With Kirsten, it's all in the imagination, the description of the feelings. That's where her passion is, not the physical, the real.

"In the beginning I did the same thing with her that you did with Alison, except that our intercourse was verbal instead of carnal; one hundred percent emotional, zero percent physical. She doesn't attach much importance to the physical act of showing your love, of making love. It just isn't important to her so she isn't very uh, very uh, accomplished or responsive." Zoey blew her nose and regained some composure. Then she shook her head back and forth rapidly. "I have an ingrained aversion memory of the first time Kirsten and I made love. We had had a romantic dinner. Eyes locked together in the candlelight. Then a walk on the beach, Kirsten whispering poetic yearnings conceived on the spot. By the time we got in bed, I was overcome with desire, in passionate expectation..."

Nora did not want to hear this. "You had an ingrained what Zoe?"

"Oh, an aversion memory. Aversion therapy is built around those, you know."

Nora wrinkled her nose and looked thoroughly puzzled, so Zoey took time to explain. She had come this far.

"This is probably not the best analogy Nora," Zoey had crawled back to safety, behind her desk. "But remember how when we first met you adored that Chic-a-Lick chicken? You had it every day for lunch or dinner."

Nora nodded, remembering. "You couldn't get enough of it. Were completely addicted to it. Until that day, I'll never forget it, when you found that gross beak! All breaded and fried up!"

"God!" they said together. They laughed and made faces and shared the memory.

"That was it for me." Nora shook her head. "I've never had a piece to this day."

"That's because it totally changed your perception. That's precisely what happened with Kirsten and me," Zoey added in a small voice. "After a couple of months, I was completely disenchanted. I found that I cared more about your unhappiness than Kirsten's happiness, and I realized then how much you meant to me. I knew I had made a big mistake, Nore."

"But why didn't you tell me? Shit, Zoey, I was going through hell."

"Why do you think? Don't you think I realized what I had done to you? I didn't want to trivialize my behavior by admitting the truth, that I was a complete idiot! I could barely admit to myself what a terrible mistake I had made, let alone admit it to others. I hated myself so much for the harm I had done, that I denied how I really felt. 'Big deal,' I told myself. 'Who needs physical passion? At my age sex loses its attraction. I can certainly do without it.' That's when I used Kirsten, pretended I was happy with her. Then there was my pride and my reputation in the community. I was the successful professional, reeking with good judgment and conscience. I didn't want the gay community or the psychological community to think I was such an unstable, frivolous shit. Besides, I knew I had blown it big time with you. I knew that I had hurt you so terribly, that you could never forgive me, let alone take me back. So, I didn't feel like I had any choice. I just hung in there with Kirsten. It hasn't been so bad. She's witty and entertaining and really quite brilliant. I just...just don't love her."

"God, Zoey!" Nora was more than stunned. "You should have come to me! Something."

"There was no way I could do that. No way to ever make you understand. Besides Gabriella already had her talons firmly embedded."

"What are you talking about! We had just met. We barely even knew each other."

"Oh, Nora, Christ!"

"Well, It's true. You're the one that introduced us."

"Not exactly. It was Kirsten. Gabriella is her attorney not mine. I remember the exact moment. I have an iconic memory of the image. I watched her shake your hand and I saw her eyes and I knew right then. Looking back on it, Kirsten probably told Gabriella that she and I had something going and I was going to break up with you. Gabriella just waited in her aerie until that happened and swooped in to the rescue. Caught you before you even hit bottom."

"She was very nice, very kind. She's the one that insisted that I see someone."

"I remember that. We met for lunch to discuss who would be best for you to see. She came along to shield you from me. She was nice, all right. Her words were nice and pleasant enough. It was her body language, the way she touched you, that was so assertive, so firmly in control."

"And professional Zoey. She was behaving in a professional capacity. Putting herself in the middle, between the two of us."

"Her language may have been professional. But her hands, the way she touched you, it was so possessive, protective and downright proprietary. Walking towards our table with you, she actually had her hand on your elbow.

Then, after you both sat down, her left hand lightly touched your right forearm every time you said a word. A couple of times she even rubbed the back of your hand."

Nora stared at her. "And you…and you remember that?" she asked incredulously.

"Vividly! I also remember Gabriella glancing at her watch and the two of you leaving first. She put an arm around you and gave you a 'there, that wasn't so bad, was it? I'm proud of you' hug. It made me want to puke.

"She made it quite clear who was with whom from that moment on."

"Funny you remember all that about how Brie touched me, and Roberta, too. How she touched my arm sometimes or hugged me. I never remember stuff like that!"

Zoey sighed and wrapped her robe tightly around her. "And the swim club masseuses and Caroline, and – God help me – even Freddie." She averted her face, unable to look at Nora as she whispered the remainder of her confession. "It's everyone and anyone Nore. I remember every time I've ever seen anyone touch you. I…I can't help it."

Blown away, Nora could do nothing but stare at Zoey as she continued.

"Of course Gabriella is the all time champ. At that concert a few weeks ago? When you had on your Dana Buchman clothes? K and I were a row in front of you and a couple of seats over. By turning my head to look at Kirsten, I could see her—Gabriella's—hand. Not only was it resting just above your knee, but it was on the inside, fingers tucked under your leg. I was mesmerized by that hand all night. Sometimes it left, only to return. Sometimes it slid up or down or gave you a squeeze. I was completely pre-occupied by it. I wanted to murder its owner, but back to our lunch. She made me wish that day, and several times since then, that I was a nun with a ruler in my hand. I would teach her, in short order, how to keep her hands to herself. It was a miracle that I was able to hold it together enough to recommend Roberta, but I did. She was fabulously successful. Everything that had been a problem was resolved. What should have been my relationship got shrunk, gift wrapped and tied with a bow. And Gabriella reaped the rewards, at least until now. I was left sinking in the quicksand of the irony. Caught in the mire, watching your life go on without me and unable to do a damn thing about it.

"Speaking of Roberta—what I told you about not needing to go back to her? All of that was true from a strictly therapeutic standpoint. But my real reason was selfish," Zoey admitted. "If you went back to her right away, then you wouldn't need me. I wanted you to need me."

"That makes me feel good, Zoey, because I do need you. I'll always need you. Roberta or no Roberta, even if she becomes my therapist again, you're my friend. Now is not the time to give up on being friends, just the opposite. I need a friend now. I really need you Zoey."

"I just can't do it, Nore. It's…it's just impossible for me. I struggle mightily not to cross that line, but I can't control it. It's almost automatic. You are impossible for me to resist," Zoey struggled to not start crying again. "I was being honest earlier, about hitting on you. In fact, my car? I could have taken it in the next day. I think I took it in when I did, on purpose so you'd have to take me home. Then, when I held you in my arms, when we were in the car, I could hardly stand it, could barely breathe. My skin yearned for your touch. I invited you in and opened two more bottles of wine, completely inappropriate behavior unless you are seducing someone. I was seducing, I guess. I think that in some stupid way I was also trying to get the courage to tell you the truth."

"You don't need to get courage from anywhere Zoey. You are made of courage. I've never known anyone who had more courage and integrity too. That's what you are made of."

Nora put her arms around Zoey then and held her while she came unglued. She thought about the two of them. She had dreamed of this moment. Zoey would realize what a terrible mistake she had made and would come crawling back to her. She would beg and cry. And Nora…Nora would get even. Nora would make her hurt every bit as much as Zoey had hurt her. But now, now that Zoey was here, actually here, in her arms and saturated with pain, things seemed so different. No longer did revenge seem so sweet. In fact, Nora was surprised to discover that it wasn't her own feelings she was concerned about at the moment.

24

"You worry too much about those so-called lines Zoe. Sure, there are rigid boundaries we all have to deal with, like the ones we have with out patients. We can't be friends with them; Not if we're going to help them; Can't even ease their pain. Most of mine come to me with mental torment as great as, or even greater than, their physical pain. They can no longer do what they used to do and they're full of inadequacies. Feel like failures.

"They're so vulnerable and they come to me for help. In order to help them, I actually have to hurt them even more. Compared to that line, the line between friends and lovers blurs. I think it's very flexible." Zoey's voice was muffled by the blanket and Nora could hardly hear her as she lay in her arms, still crying, but still trying to explain.

"I'm not talking about a line separating friends and lovers. With me, it's a constant effort to cross over to the right side and then sliding back again to the wrong side. It's more like a barrier, a big wall that I have to get over. It takes a certain amount of time and everything I have to scale it. Then, when I finally get to the top and I'm ready to descend to the other side, the land of innocent friendship, you telephone me. Your voice sounds shaky. I can tell by the way you say my name that something is wrong; Or our eyes meet at a party. We exchange a glance, each knowing exactly what the other is thinking; Or you smile at me over dinner, a wistful, longing, 'if only' smile. And I'm back suddenly, back at the bottom of the wall. I race to meet you, to see why your voice sounds like that; Or I follow up that exchanged glance with a pithy comment, 'I see you still can't resist brie and sun-dried tomatoes' or better yet…'this feels so wrong.'"

"God! I do that to you? I don't mean to! It sounds so manipulative. I'll try not to. I'm so sorry Zoe. Tell me what to do and I'll do it. I'll do anything to keep you as a friend, anything. Maybe we should change the rules. Only meet in public. Never be alone together, that sort of thing."

"Is that what you want?" Zoey looked down at her, her tears falling on Nora's face.

"No. God no!" Nora clutched desperately at the bed covers. "But I'll do anything to keep from losing you completely. Is that what you want?...to just not see each other at all anymore?" The very thought made Nora panic, her skin prickling with fear.

"No. That's not what I want." Zoey wiped her tears off Nora's nose. "I realized tonight that we're stuck on the other side of that line or barricade or whatever it is. We started out on that side and that's where we've always been. We've always been lovers, never friends. Ex-lovers maybe, but never just friends. We don't have any of the expectations that a friendship involves and we don't have the boundaries either. Those boundaries don't exist on our side of the line. And I'm not going to struggle anymore to try being something I'm not. I can't change who I am, or who you are, or the history we have. And I can't change what happens between us, how we react to each other, either. So I'm just not going to fight it anymore."

"But why Zoe? Why can't ex-lovers be friendly? I don't get it!"

"I didn't say ex-lovers can't be friendly. Of course they can. They can be pleasant and polite and get along very well. Maybe some of them can make the switch, over time, to love each other as friends. I don't think we can, Nora. I know I can't."

"I don't understand what you mean, I guess."

"I mean, Nore, that it's a totally different relationship. Friends want to help each other feel better when they are hurting, be there for each other. When you are hurting I want to make you feel better. I want to be the cause of your feeling better. I want to love you in such a way as to cure you of the hurt. Friends want to be happy and have a good time together. I want to make you happy, to be the reason for your happiness."

Nora looked at her doubtfully. "No shit?"

Zoey nodded solemnly. "No shit," she vowed in a whisper, closing her eyes. "Besides friends do not caress each other's faces or seek comfort enveloped in each others' arms like we do. They have boundaries that we just don't have."

"Well, of course. Everyone knows that. I just don't get what you mean Zoey? I don't see where you're going." Nora was totally confused.

"I mean, Nore, that when you call and ask if we can get together – know that you're calling a lover. When you smile longingly or look knowingly at me, know that I'm a lover, not a friend. Because that's what I am Nore, and I can't help it and I can't change it. Also, if I ask you to stay here, to stay with me instead of at Sybil's you have to understand that I'm asking you as a lover, not a friend."

"Are…are you asking me that?"

Zoey nodded.

"I mean, no shit? You really would let me stay here?" Nora was dumbfounded.

"Stay was a poor word to choose." Zoey took a deep breath. "I should have said, 'live.' It has less of a temporary connotation."

Nora sat straight up. "You're asking me to move in?"

"Yes. I'm asking you to live with me. Like I said, not as a friend, as a lover."

"An ex-lover, you mean."

Zoey put a finger across Nora's lips. "If you say so Nore. That's up to you. You're calling the shots here. That's what I have been trying to tell you. I never thought I'd have this chance, and after what I did to you, I don't have the right to ask you to forgive me or to trust me. I don't even have the right to ask you to forget everything and begin anew. But I've been obsessing on what you said the other night about how much we both have changed and how maybe we could make it work. I'd give anything to give that a try, really anything. But I don't have that right, Nore. I can only tell you how I feel. Wait, don't say anything. Please let me finish while I still have the courage. I love you Nora and right now that's the most important thing in the world to me. I think I've known this for some time but I guess I didn't have the nerve to acknowledge it, let alone tell you. Every time I see you it's like ripping the scab off of an old wound. I realize once again, how I hurt you and the heartache that wells up within me is killing me, literally killing me. Sometimes I get physically ill; really sick, for a few days. I thought it was hopeless. How could I ever make you understand how I feel? How full of sorrow and regret I am. And it was hopeless Nore." Zoey's voice quavered, "until you did the same thing to Gabriella that I did to you. Now I know that at least you can understand…understand all of it. The temptation; giving in to it, hating yourself for doing that and yet doing it anyway. And the hurt. Causing that unbearable hurt, betraying the trust, inflicting such pain, wreaking such chaos. Then, finally, suffering through the regret, the endless regret that permeates your existence. It affects everything around you."

The warning signals in Nora's head became nuclear attack alerts. After all, this was the woman who almost did her in five years ago. "I don't know, Zoey. I'm so scared. Scared to trust you."

"I know that Nore. I can't expect you to trust me or to forgive me, either. Trust and forgiveness need to be earned. I'm only telling you the truth. Telling you how I feel. I owe you that much and I need for you to know where I am. Who knows, maybe it will bring you some satisfaction. Or help you make sense of what happened between us.

Maybe you can feel compassion for me now, instead of being so bitter. If you can, then maybe it will help me heal. I'd do anything to try to make it up to you. Anything I could to make you happy." Her voice was becoming raspy and she sobbed out of control, her body quaking and shuddering. All of her pain had risen to the surface and she didn't know what to do with it. She was used to dealing with this sort of thing from a totally opposite perspective. Now, like a pitcher trying to hit a fast ball, all of her training and knowledge were worthless.

Nora was shocked, or in shock! This was all breaking news to her. She had no idea. Nora knew Zoey loved her, but she really thought they were friends, the best of friends. Clueless. Nora guessed she really was clueless.

She played for time. "But what about you? Could you ever trust me after what I did to Gabriella? I don't think I would trust me!"

Zoey pulled some tissues out of her robe pocket. She wiped off her face and blew her nose. "That was a two way street, Nora. She rejected you. She practically pushed you into bed with Alison. She left you wanting more, over and over again, because she was satisfied. Satisfied but selfish." Zoey looked at Nora for a long time. "It doesn't excuse what you did to her. But you have to realize, honey, it really was a two way street. It wasn't all your fault. Who knows, maybe Gabriella unconsciously rejected you because she wanted out. I bet she never did that in the beginning. When you were 'new' together."

No. She didn't, Nora admitted to herself. It wasn't that she was so unhappy with Gabriella, miserable or anything. Most of the time things were okay. Not like when she had been with Zoey, but still okay. Different, but okay. But there were times, other times, when she felt suffocated, overwhelmed, in over her head, so taken for granted, so depended on, so trapped. "The calendar," she said aloud. "Brie keeps a five year calendar. I'm not sure why, but it makes me sick to my stomach to look at it."

Zoey took her hand in both of her own. "It's a tangible manifestation of

Gabriella's plans and expectations. Your reaction indicates your resistance to being a part of those plans and expectations and your growing desperation to get out."

"It doesn't take away how I feel though. I feel so awful Zoe."

"I know, sweetheart. I feel awful, too. I have for four years. The worst part of my pain goes away. Sometimes it gets buried by other stuff. But then, when it returns, it takes me by surprise and I discover that it has lost none of its intensity, no matter how much time has passed."

"So you still feel as bad as you did when we first split? As bad as I do right now?"

Zoey nodded. "The shared pain of the true shits of the world." She smiled, but she couldn't quite manage the grin. "Honestly though, I never could have told you before because I had never owned these feelings, Nore. Some therapist, huh!"

Nora tried to understand. "So tonight…just tonight you figured this all out?"

"It was in there. It was all in there. Has been for a long time. Tonight I took responsibility. I came clean; first to myself, and then to you. A big part of it was this weekend and then all of those messages. I got in bed and listened to them over and over in my head. Why didn't I feel worse about Kirsten? I'm sure, like I told you, I can make her understand. But 'hey!' I thought. 'Maybe this is actually a good thing. As long as everyone thinks there is something going on between Nora and me, maybe I should ask Nora to move in.'

"Then I thought about you, these last four days and Ritchy and Ellie. A three year old child was able to zero in on my neediness. How pathetic is that? I must exude it."

"So, just because everyone thinks we're together, you're asking me to move in?" Zoey nodded and Nora went on with a laugh. "You're using me, in other words, to break up with Kirsten."

"Shamelessly," Zoey nodded in agreement. "Also, shamelessly—I have no shame, I can't afford shame—I want you here, Nore. I want you back so much."

Zoey started crying again. "I haven't even thought about a baby for years. It has to do with you Nore. I've kept all my emotion, all my yearning, all my caring, all my loving, under strict control since we were together. Now, four days with you and I'm a mess.

"Then I tried to think what I wanted, really wanted. Was it a house with a fence around it and a yard full of kids and dogs? Is that what this baby thing is all about? No. I decided I don't care so much about any of that right now. At the moment all I care about is you. I can't get past that to even think of kids and dogs and picket fences. I am totally obsessed with trying to undo what I did to you…and…and I want to love you, Nore. Physically, I mean. I am so God damn tired of talking about love. Having weeks, maybe months, go bye without feeling the touch of another person. No wonder I went bananas holding Ritchy. No wonder I clung to Ellie like that. When we heard Kirsten's message earlier, and you hugged me…I doubt if you even realized you did. It was so off-hand, spontaneous, nothing heavy, almost superficial. Just meant to show support. Still, it made me realize how much I needed to be hugged, held in someone's arms."

Zoey stopped. She took a deep breath and squared her shoulders, her eyes never leaving Nora's. "So, I woke you up to tell you how I feel and ask you to please stay here. I could pretend to you that we'd just be friends and roommates, but I can't promise that Nore. The shrink inside me won't let me do that.

"I can promise that I'll let you call the shots no matter what I'm feeling inside. I'm taking the biggest chance of my life here. Taking a chance and asking for a chance I guess. And I haven't a clue how I would handle rejection, a rejection that would be poetic justice.

"Still, I tell my patients every day…if you don't ask for what you want, chances are you're never going to get it. I've learned that life really is short. It goes on while we sit around regretting and longing. I just can't sit around doing that any longer. I can't. I can't promise that you'll ever trust me like you once did, but I can promise that I'll never betray you again. Never! Where I'm coming from doesn't have a lot to do with me. How I feel about this or that. Or, even how what you do makes me feel. It's not about me anymore. That ache I have won't let it be about me. All I truly care about is you. Please let me prove it to you. Please Nore."

"We could go back to calling each other all day on the phone. I could check up on you that way while you're earning my trust and forgiveness." Nora pulled Zoey's face close and she could see the relief in her eyes when she said it. It was the first humorous, and therefore encouraging, thing Nora had said.

Zoey kissed her ever so softly, tentatively. Her eyes penetrated Nora's, searching for acceptance. "And I promise, Nore, I'll never leave you like that, unfulfilled like that…never."

"Well now, that is a commitment."

"Especially from one who knows what she's getting into." Zoey nuzzled her neck. "Oh God Nore. Oh God I've missed this, missed you so."

Nora wanted to cover all the bases. "But speaking of commitments, you know how you are Zoe, and you and Kirsten are really still together. Aren't you going to feel shitty cheating on her? You know you will."

Zoey kissed her again then. It was a long, long, longing kiss, longed for…for a long, long time. It left Nora breathless. "As far as Kirsten and I are concerned, we've been lingering over dessert after a multi-course meal. Neither one of us wanted to finish first. And neither one of us wanted the responsibility of picking up the check and signifying that's it's over. It has been over for a while, really, and it doesn't have anything to do with you. Unless…" Zoey stopped in mid-thought, her body frozen in place along with her voice.

"Unless what?" Nora wouldn't let it go.

"Well, unless it was all about you always from the beginning." Zoey said slowly. "Shit! K probably saw that, knew that, knew it all along. That's why she always got so furious at the mention of your name. She knew I never stopped loving you."

Nora held her breath.

"Besides," Zoey whispered in her ear, "there is only one honorable reason for breaking a commitment and that is a prior commitment." She began to kiss Nora's eyelids and nose and forehead and cheeks. And she whispered between these kisses. "And that's what we have here, a prior commitment. I'll never hurt you again, Nora. I promise. No don't…don't. You don't need to promise anything, only that you'll talk to me. That's all I ask. Give me a chance and just please talk to me."

25

Nora searched Zoey's face, looking deep into her eyes; looking for answers to questions she hadn't had time to formulate yet. Like, what the shit is going on here?

Zoey had said Wednesday night that they needed to get their past behind them. In the car, she had held Nora in her arms and patted her on the back and told her to try to forgive herself and just move on. And then once they got to Zoey's she had unloaded all those reasons; big and small, right and wrong, why she had broken up with her. Now she was saying those reasons were bull. *Why? What really happened between us?* Nora wondered.

Well, first, hearing about Alison really did force her to remember how we were when we were together. Then, learning what I did to Brie. That was big. She figured that my perspective of her dumping me would have to change. I would have to be more understanding.

As for all those bullshit reasons she brought up, they are not really bullshit. It's just that they aren't applicable anymore. They no longer exist, and Zoey knows it. Maybe that was really Zoey's way of pointing out to me how much we've both changed. Allowing me to then come to the obvious conclusion.

Funny, up until tonight I always thought Zoey had it all together. Never realized that she was insecure, too. She always seemed so squared away. I was so young, so immature. I expected her to be mature, secure and responsible for both of us. I put her in charge because I thought she knew all the answers. But she didn't want that. She didn't want to be in charge at all. Part of the attraction to Kirsten was that she became the frivolous, spontaneous, fun loving one.

Maybe, after Zoey and Brie, that was part of my attraction to Alison. She was so young, in so many ways. It forced me into a new roll, the mature, stable, decision-maker. I didn't much like it, but it made me realize I don't want either one of those rolls. I've grown out of both of 'em. Maybe you have to take a shot at each one to learn how to share being both. I'm pretty sure that's how Zoey feels, too. She wants an equal relationship. She doesn't want to be adored and idolized, she just wants the reciprocal give and take of mature love, those tiny advances and retreats that are part of being partners in love.

Under the veneer of control though, there sure lurks an entirely different Zoey and I never knew she existed. Brie was so damaged, so vulnerable; and Alison was so damaged, so vulnerable. Is it possible that Zoey was the same? Her shot about my being a nurturer. Was that why we were attracted to each other too? Was she damaged and vulnerable and needy too?

I was always so loved, so secure and happy growing up. It never occurred to me that maybe Zoey wasn't. Then, up at the cabin she told me about her parents: how she hated going to the Lake, how unhappy she and Joan were, how crappy her dad has been, a long ago hurt but kept well hidden, safe and protected. She sure isn't close to her family. Not like I am. She's so much more self-sufficient – or is that isolated. Her sister has been seeing Willy for all that time and Zoey didn't even know it. If she's that removed from her own family and Kirsten is so emotionally absent...then Zoey must really feel alone. That's the price she has had to pay for hiding and protecting those old hurts. She can't afford to be close to her family. She doesn't even have close friends. Not like I do. She chalks it up to her job and she's right, of course. At least partially right. Obviously, she has to shut down her own emotions to do what she does, but it's awfully convenient, too. And what about Kirsten? Intellectually emotional but really self-absorbed. She fit in perfectly to Zoey's well-ordered psyche until...well, I guess until the last few days. If Zoey and I had never met for dinner Wednesday night, none of the rest of this would have happened. And she and Kirsten would still be together, lingering over the meal and reluctant to end it.

So what happened? Why the big one-eighty here? No question that being with me and my family and living through our trauma was a large contributor, but Zoey's loss of control was 'an inside job' as we say at work. At work I would call this a break through. My patients come to me in denial; even the ones who claim to accept whatever new limitations they're experiencing due to the event that changed their lives; Even the most positive, cheerful ones. Before they can heal they have to know in their gut that things are not the same. They can't continue doing what they did. That gut knowledge is the breakthrough. In some ways this is where Zoey is right now.

I know this woman, I know her like I know myself. She doesn't say things she doesn't believe with all her heart and when she discovers that something she said was wrong, she is quick to make it right. That's the thing about Zoey. She is always quick to correct herself. Always. Just like tonight. She has a real reverence for the truth. Her integrity and honor finally dragged her out from behind her desk. Now here she is without the armor of her authority and the security of her knowledge, reduced to tears, vulnerable and exposed and letting me see it all.

We've been through a lot together and, of course, I've seen Zoey crying and emotional. But I have never seen her like this. Never. It isn't like her and that's why I am positive that she really is completely and thoroughly out of control.

Then Nora saw Zoey's eyes brimming over. Those windows to that soul that demanded so much of itself; so much courage, strength, honor and virtue. Nora knew in that moment she could never disappoint or betray those eyes again.

Finally, she spoke. "I have to give you the chance, Zoe. I promised Ellie I would try. I told myself at the time that I only said that to shut her up. I really did mean it though. At least I meant that I would try if I had the chance." Nora smiled ruefully. "I didn't even imagine, of course, I'd ever have that chance. But if I'm going to try, I need you to try something too."

"Anything! I promise! I'll…"

Nora interrupted her. "I don't want to start over, go back to how things were before. I'm not the same and neither are you. I don't even want to move in here, but I will temporarily."

Nora now had Zoey's rapt attention. "What?" She waited, holding her breath for Nora to go on.

"Zoey!" Nora took her hands. "I've always deferred to your expertise in matters related to your work. Now It's your turn to defer to me."

Zoey froze, eyes huge, not knowing what to expect.

"I think you've had a real breakthrough Zoe. Occupationally, that is. I think you are at the point where you can't repress your emotions any more. Oh, I'm sure being the professional that you are, you can get back to doing so. But, why? Why Zoey? Why take up the struggle again? You said yourself that you didn't want to become what the job was turning you into. Well, what I'm trying to say is that I don't want to be with you if you become like that.

I love you the way you are right now…honest and real, and a total mess. So call that guy at the University and tell him you'll take the job, for Christ sake!"

"But what about my patients? The altruism I told you about."

"If you're really determined to follow the most altruistic path, that with the most benefit for the most people, the University job has the potential of benefitting many more people. You see what, ten? Fifteen patients at a time?"

"About…if that…usually less than fifteen."

"Well, if you only had ten students and each one of them went on to have ten patients," Nora raised her eyebrows, "and that's only for one year."

Zoey looked ambivalent. "I feel so responsible, though."

"I'm sure you do. That's one of the reasons I love you. Keep the patients you have then, if you want to. Just don't take any new ones. We can use the time while you're scaling back to fix this place up and sell it and buy something out by the University. A place that belongs to both of us."

"You're into renovating all of a sudden?" Zoey smiled thinly. "This place, my career…us."

"Mostly us, Zoe. I'm willing to give it a try but my expertise tells me you have about had it as a therapist. The bad so far outweighs the good for you. If that comes to a crises I don't want it to involve you and me, our relationship. Besides, I feel like I need to make a move right now. I love you too much to let you go on feeling like this. I guess that's what it's about, huh! What love is about. Risking my own vulnerability to ease yours. Exposing myself to heartache and hurt again, to help soothe yours. Kind of like what you just woke me up to do, huh."

They kissed again, a slow, restrained, exploring kind of kiss that turned hungry and urgent and passionate.

"Thank God." Zoey could barely talk. "Oh, thank you, baby, thank you, thank you. We'll move. I'll call Cole right away! You're right. In my heart I know it."

"Well," Nora whispered. "It is my job."

"Oh Nore you can't know, can't imagine. I need you baby. Oh, God, I need you so much."

"You called me 'Baby.'"

"I did? Yeah, I guess I did."

"You haven't called me that for a long, long time."

Zoey buried her face in Nora's hair. "Probably not. I don't…I don't remember calling you that."

"It was when we were new, brand new. Before I moved in, and maybe for a little while after. You used to study in here, in this room."

"God! That's right. I'd forgotten all about that. I had Dad's old leather couch from his office and the roll-top desk was over there." Zoey leaned on one elbow and pointed.

"And I called you Zwee, remember? Zoey without the o. I would finish whatever I was doing and get ready for bed and then I would stand in the doorway and beg you in baby talk."

"Pweez Zwee," they both said at once.

"Sometimes you would come to bed, but sometimes you would pat the couch next to you." Nora ran her hands up Zoey's arms and looked up at her. "And then you would hold me in your arms, just like a baby. You called me Baby. You held me with one arm and a textbook with your other hand and you read aloud to me…'the axon carries the signals between the dendrites and the terminal buttons.' It might as well have been Chinese for all I knew. All I knew was I was there, in your arms, and I couldn't get close enough."

"And I called you Baby?"

"All the time. 'You understand Baby? About the axon? About what it does? You see, Baby, how one external locus of control can be either healthy or harmful?' Or sometimes, I couldn't stand it and I would try to get something going and you would say, 'Please, Baby. Be a good Baby now and let me get through this. Just one more hour, Baby, okay?'"

They stared at each other and nodded, remembering. "Why did we get rid of that old couch?"

"A misguided attempt at keeping up appearances on my part," Zoey acknowledged. "When you moved in, I thought it was important for you to have your own room. So we got this bed and I moved my desk upstairs to the— 'bonus room,'" they finished in unison their sarcastic imitation of the real estate agent's official description of the area.

"What happened to the couch Zoe?"

"I gave it to Joan, along with the roll-top desk. That's when I got the office system, remember? And the entertainment center."

"That's when you got rid of the 'baby' too, Zoe. You stopped studying on the couch, stopped holding me like that, stopped calling me 'baby,' started studying upstairs. And I stopped begging, Pweez Zwee!"

"And that was just about the time I got 'the baby thing' the first time. Christ, Nore! How stupid can I get. It wasn't just that I wanted a baby. I wanted my baby. I wanted my baby back! I had found a way to study and have you at the same time and I was too stupid to know it. I locked myself away from you and the 'baby thing' erupted. God, Nore! Don't let me do it again! It's you, baby. You are my 'baby thing.' And I need you, need you just to survive."

Nora heard Zoey whisper that, and her universe exploded on the spot. She knew then, beyond all doubt. Zoey had never said that to a living soul and never would admit such a thing unless she was desperate.

Nora saw stars – literally. She threw off the covers and, on her knees, threw Zoey's robe on top of them.

Their eyes met and, with perfect clarity, exchanged one of those knowing glances. In slow motion, Nora pulled her close.

"It's like I told you Zoe. You're my one and only...always and forever. I've never loved anyone the way I love you." Nora cradled her tenderly, protecting her, holding something fragile and precious.

Zoey's tears became a constant flow...a river. They mixed with Nora's own. Each one barely believed the other was really there, and this was really happening. They clung to each other for the confirmation they needed and they cried. God, but they cried! The dam they had constructed had held for four years. For four long years it had held in hurt, and sorrow and bitterness and unshed tears. Now that it had burst they were engulfed; flooded by those tears; cleansing them and washing away the pollution of pride.

Nora was content to just hold Zoey, to feel her body. She could feel her arms and legs and knees and elbows. And, it was as if she could feel the two of them coming together again, becoming one, again. Nora's right hand slid down Zoey's left arm, to her hand. She touched the ring. "It's called an eternity ring," she whispered in Zoey's ear.

"I lied about the flea collar bit. I've never taken it off," Zoey admitted. Her hands began to move slowly and reverently over Nora's body, repossessing it. As they moved they set the skin beneath them on fire.

"Oh God. Oh God Nore. It's been so long. I've ached for this moment Baby."

"Zoe, it's the middle of the night. Maybe we should, you know, cool it. Don't you have to give your report on the seminar tomorrow?"

"Peace of cake. No-brainer. I could do it in my sleep. I have total command of the subject matter." Zoey looked down at her. "Recognizing and managing unconscious triggers to Defense Mechanisms – including: repression, regression, denial, projection, hallucination, compensation, sublimation, and rationalization," she recited with an absolutely straight face.

Then she flashed Nora that grin. It illuminated the whole world, well not really the whole world, but all of it that really mattered. And in that flash, Nora got it, really got it. *This is it, our world. This is all of it. Nobody else and nothing else matters. We are our world. All Zoey wants to do is love me, that's absolutely all. And all I want, or need, is to love her, too. We just didn't know how at first. We didn't understand what love really is. Didn't understand about the giving instead of getting or the 'unselfish risking' involved.*

Nora could see too that, sometimes when you just can't get over someone, can't get past your past with them, well, maybe that's the point. Maybe you're not supposed to.

Nora kissed her again to show her how she felt. She still wasn't that great at verbalizing. Besides, after Kirsten, Nora thought that was the last thing Zoey needed right then. Aflame with desire, she gave all of herself to Zoey in that kiss. She held nothing back. "This...now this feels right!" she told her.

* * * * *